FIX FRIDA

SHEILA HOLYER

Tellwell Talent
www.tellwell.ca

ISBN
978-0-2288-9074-4 (Hardcover)
978-0-2288-9073-7 (Paperback)
978-0-2288-9075-1 (eBook)

To everyone out there, young and old,
who is trying to figure things out.

TABLE OF CONTENTS

COURAGE

I was my bravest at two years old. I left the house where I lived with my mom Arlene and a bunch of other people. I just walked out the door and wandered off on my own. Someone found me in a farmer's field with just my diaper in mid-March. There was still snow on the ground. Arlene didn't realize that I had left the house.

Years later I read the social worker's report. Whoever found me didn't know where I lived, and I couldn't tell them since I was just two. They called the police. Eventually the police figured out where I belonged, but it must have been clear that things were not too good in that house for a child. The social worker's report was grim. "...illicit drug use.... open bottles of alcohol .... unsanitary." I understood all that. There was one word in the report that I didn't know: "contrite" ... "mother is contrite..." I had to look it up.

I marvel now at how brave I must have been to walk out of that house. I'm sure I did it because I knew I wasn't safe there. I don't have clear memories of that time, just a shadow of a feeling of fear, and the sour smell of spilled beer. When I think about little two-year-old me striking out across the farmer's field, I feel amazed and proud.

I guess because Arlene was "contrite" and tried to make some changes, it took a few years before the Children's Aid was able to take me for good and give me to Harold and Maggie. With Harold and Maggie I didn't need to be brave. They were responsible. They took care of things for me, and I didn't need the survival instincts that had driven me out the door. At least I didn't need them for a few years.

When Sandra and I met we were both twelve. I was drawn to her from the first moment I saw her. It was the first day she started at Thornton Middle School in North York. I would usually move down the hallways with my head down just trying to get from one class to another without having to really interact with anyone. I had perfected the art of invisibility. Whatever friends I had had at elementary school had found new groups and somehow I had gotten left out in the intricate shuffling of partners, like an inexperienced dancer who finds herself outside the patterns and formations of a square dance.

The day I met Sandra I stopped in the hallway because she was there at the centre of a group of kids who were grilling her about which school she had come from.

"St. Margaret's?" said Felicia, a grade-eight tough-girl who was regularly caught smoking in the girls' bathroom. "What's that? A Catholic school?" Her disdain was clear.

"Why do you Catholic school girls wear your skirts so short? It's slutty," added Cathy, Felicia's sidekick. Everyone looked at Sandra to determine whether this "Catholic-school slut" label could fit. Sandra was a little shorter than the grade eights, so she had to look up to meet their eyes, which she did. Her brown hair hung straight and thick to her mid-back, and her eyelashes were longer and darker than real life eyelashes should really be. She was wearing a little lip gloss, but otherwise no makeup. She was definitely good looking.

Sandra stood still while they grilled her. She held her ground standing with both feet firmly planted in the middle of the hallway and not allowing them to edge her up against the lockers. She didn't blush or try to escape. She was the opposite of invisible. I felt nervous for her, and the way she crossed her arms that made me wonder if she wasn't more nervous than she was letting on. I didn't have the nerve to intervene, but I couldn't look away. I shouldn't have worried. Sandra was more than equal to a little name-calling from Cathy and Felicia.

She one-upped them, "Slutty? You're not kidding. So many girls I know from St. Margaret's already got pregnant."

Cathy and Felicia had no response. The bell rang and Cathy and Felicia moved on laughing and jostling down the hall. Sandra was left trying to open her locker.

"My name is Frida," I told her, "Do you have science next?" I guess the adrenaline from standing up to the grade eight questioning had faded because Sandra was a little shaky when she answered.

"I'm not sure. This is my first day."

I saw the pink paper that the school used for timetables amongst her things. "Can I just look at your timetable?" I saw that she was in science and I didn't have anyone sitting beside me in class. "You do have science. Let's go together and you can sit by me." Sandra looked at me, and for some reason she decided that yes, she would be friends with this skinny girl. That was the beginning.

Sandra was magic. When I was with her, I felt the world firm up and take on interesting contours and colours where before there was just a fog and shifting shapes. It was small things that made her so magic, but there was no denying her power. Sandra knew all the words to the rap section of "Airplanes". She seemed to know them before the rest of us even heard the song, and way before it was a hit. After going to see *Attack the Block* she could do a flawless South London accent and we would re-enact scenes from the movie after school. The day in gym class that I got my first period, it was Sandra that got me clean shorts and a pad and covered up my late arrival in class by pelting Susie Broderick in the head with a volleyball.

Being friends with Sandra was the best thing about my life. Even now, more than ten years after we first met, I catch myself looking at people and situations and movies and clothes as I imagine Sandra would look at them. As Sandra and I would have looked at them. Before the shooting. Before Brian. Before I betrayed her.

VACUUM CLEANERS

———————— ı|ı ————————

When I came to live with Harold and Maggie I had never seen a vacuum cleaner. There were a lot of things about Harold and Maggie's house that seemed strange: regular meals, a quiet comfortable bedroom with clean sheets, music playing on the radio in the kitchen, but the vacuum cleaner really freaked me out.

It was an old Hoover with a long grey hose that looked snake-like to my five-year-old eyes. I heard Maggie running it on maybe the second day that I lived with them. My brain couldn't understand what was going on. The noise, the snake-like hose, the bizarre thrusting movements Maggie was making to operate the thing. I must have looked terrified.

"What is it, Frida?" said Maggie, turning off the Hoover.

I couldn't speak. I didn't know what to say or ask. My nightmares were populated by adults who seemed to be human but then would be revealed as gorillas or robots. A part of me thought maybe this was a nightmare coming true. Maggie was a robot, or she was controlling this robot thing.

"It's just a vacuum, Frida. We use it to clean the carpet. See – when I run it over here it gets nice and clean." Maggie showed me how it plugged in and how to tug on the power cord just so to get it to retract with surprising force. The whole thing was terrifying, and although I could see that the carpet was clean after passing over it, the pile all combed satisfyingly in one direction, I wasn't sure that it was worth it. The vacuum cleaner lived in the cupboard under the stairs. I had to steel myself for a possible glimpse of the snake-like hose when I went in there to get toilet paper or a dusting cloth.

Eventually I got over my fear of the vacuum cleaner, but I recognized something like it in Sandra when she came over after school. Maggie was running the vacuum. She loved to vacuum, that woman. She had made snacks for us to eat. As she ate, Sandra watched Maggie and that vacuum cleaner with rapt attention. It wasn't fear – we were twelve by then and Sandra, I knew, was not fearful by nature. But she was perplexed, fascinated. I had a feeling I knew why. My feeling was confirmed a few weeks later when I went to Sandra's house for the first time.

The house itself was a normal suburban house. The paint was peeling and the garden was overgrown. Sandra didn't go in through the front door. She walked up to the front corner of the house where there was a small window at ground level. The window was cracked and dirty and partly obscured by weeds, but Sandra knocked on it nonchalantly and then motioned for me to follow her around to the side door. We waited there until her mom came to let us in.

Sandra lived with her mom in the basement of the house. Harold and Maggie's basement was full of junk and featured wood panelling, vinyl flooring and pervasive dampness, but Sandra's basement home was cement floor, wood joists and an old laundry sink that seemed to be serving as the kitchen sink.

I couldn't fully absorb that this was where Sandra lived, or that there could be something wrong with the fact that this is where Sandra lived because Sandra scuttled around quickly grabbing whatever she came to pick up and then we left. I met her mom and she seemed confused, mildly surprised maybe that Sandra had brought home a friend. There might have been a brief exchange of words between Sandra and her mom. I might have been introduced. I don't remember. But I am 100% sure that there was no vacuum cleaner in that basement apartment.

Sandra and I never discussed where she lived and it never occurred to me that her living conditions meant that she was lacking something because Sandra was magic. Everyone knew it. Just like the time she wanted to go to the beach.

THE BEACH

————— ı|ıı —————

It was the summer before we started high school, Sandra
wanted to go to the beach. Of course we could get to
Cherry Beach by TTC, or Ward's Island beach by TTC and
Toronto Island Ferry, but Sandra had got it in her head that we
should go to Wasaga Beach, and the only way to get there was
to drive, and of course we didn't have a car or a driver's license.

I don't know how Sandra even got the idea of Wasaga Beach
in her mind, but once she had an idea of something she wanted
to do, it was pretty hard to dissuade her. Not only could I not
get her to forget about doing something that she wanted to do,
she could convince me to do all sorts of things I didn't really
want to do and, more often than not, convince me that I was
enjoying myself. And the funny thing is, I did enjoy myself. I
never would have done half the things I did had it not been for
Sandra.

People always wanted to be around Sandra. I had the
privilege of being the chosen partner of most of her exploits,
even if, as I said before, I had to be talked into most of them.

So, the beach. How were we going to get there? I told Harold and Maggie that Sandra's mom was going to take us, but Sandra's mom didn't have a car, and anyway she had to work weekends. Sandra had a plan.

"Steve has a car," she told me. I couldn't think for a second who Steve was, but then I remembered she had mentioned this older guy Steve that she knew from before she moved to our neighbourhood. When she had mentioned him before it was during a conversation about shaving legs.

"Steve used to feel all the girls' legs to see who had shaved properly," Sandra told me. I had trouble picturing this. Would all the girls line up for inspection by Steve? Why was he the one given the power to decide who had done a good job and who had not? I also knew that my legs would likely not pass Steve's inspection since Maggie was not too big on teaching me those "lady grooming" things. Any personal care beyond brushing my hair and brushing my teeth, which Maggie encouraged me to do, was pretty much left for me to figure out. The mysteries of leg and underarm shaving, eyebrow plucking and fingernail painting were beyond my understanding.

So Steve the leg smoothness expert had a car. Would he be willing to drive us to Wasaga Beach? Sandra seemed to think she could convince him. I believed her.

Sandra's old neighbourhood was right downtown. Queen Street East, east of any place I had ever been on Queen Street: the Eaton Centre, Nathan Phillips Square. We rode the Yonge line to Queen and then the 501 Queen car east past St. Michael's Hospital, past the men's shelters and run down store fronts, over the Don River until we got to the 7-11 at the corner of Queen and Brooklyn. This is where Steve could reliably be found, Sandra told me. Especially in the afternoons because later in the evening he would go to work at the gas station still further east.

Sure enough, he was there. Leaning up against the front of his car with a few young people milling around drinking

Slurpees and smoking cigarettes. Smoking cigarettes was something I was not very good at yet. Sandra was trying to teach me, but I was having a hard time looking cool while coughing and turning green and feeling like I wanted to puke.

Steve was maybe twenty years old, but that seemed really old to us. He had two of the magic "adult" signifiers: a car and a job.

He recognized Sandra right away, even though she had moved out of the neighbourhood more than a year ago and had only visited once or twice since then.

"You just missed Alicia," he said by way of greeting. He looked at me for maybe three seconds.

"Is she still going out with Raymond?" asked Sandra. Steve and the two or three other young people gathered around laughed at this question, but it was the perfect question to ask since it established Sandra as someone in the know. Not only did she know Alicia (I did not), she knew that Alicia had been dating Raymond (obviously I did not know this either).

This intimate knowledge of some key neighbourhood people was enough to enable Sandra to join the group by Steve's car effortlessly, and since I came with her, I more or less was allowed to slip in too. I did a lot of slipping in alongside Sandra.

"Steve, you ever been to Wasaga Beach?" asked Sandra when it was getting late and we would soon need to be heading back north.

"Oh yeah! Great beach. Haven't been there in a while though."

"Yeah, well Frida and I thought we would go this weekend."

Steve looked impressed. "Probably be a good party there this weekend. I might go myself."

"Oh definitely, everybody's going to be there!" said Sandra, with a cool drag on her cigarette. "We could ride with you."

And just like that we had a ride to Wasaga Beach. I wondered if Steve knew that we had come all the way downtown to ask for a ride to Wasaga Beach. If he knew we had no other way to get there. I had a feeling that he still would have offered to drive us. Steve watched Sandra attentively as she talked with other people in the group. He shifted his leaning position on the front of his car slightly so that Sandra could prop herself beside him. Everyone else in the group stood with nothing to lean on, just milling and jockeying for position.

Steve drove us to Wasaga Beach in his Toyota. Steve got a ticket for failing to stop at a stop sign. This made him rail against "stupid pigs" until we got on the highway and the monotony seemed to lull him. When he got quiet, Sandra and I came to life singing and laughing as the Toyota cruised up the 400 past Barrie. Finally we arrived. Steve parked the car and we walked to the beach. We lounged on the sand, turning over periodically to ensure even tanning. Steve got into a fight with a guy at the hot dog stand and got a cut above his eye. This put him in a sour mood again.

"Fuckin' country-hick asshole." He told us when we asked what happened to his eye. The cut was bleeding and the blood was getting into his eye. He tried wiping it away with the towel, but that was full of sand, so it just made things worse. "I got some kleenex in the car." He motioned for Sandra to go with him.

Sandra looked at me, "you better stay and watch our stuff."

The day was hot. The beach was full. I looked at the other girls and women to compare myself. The only ones skinnier than me were young girls who were still building sand castles and running unselfconsciously in and out of the water. I might have dozed off a little because when I started to wonder what was taking Steve and Sandra so long, the light had started to change, the sun shifted slightly lower in the sky. Finally I saw Sandra walking towards me. Steve followed at a bit of a distance. Sandra looked different. Her face was a little mottled and she was holding the top of her bathing suit as she walked like she was afraid it would fall off. Anyone who didn't know Sandra like I did would not have noticed. She still drew eyes as she walked. She was still magic; but, just like the first day I met her and saw those crossed arms, I knew she was not in her full power. She didn't look at me when she arrived at our spot. She didn't want to talk. She rolled herself in her towel and lay on her side facing away from me and Steve.

The cut over Steve's eye had stopped bleeding. It still looked pretty bad, but he didn't complain. He drank one of the beers he had brought in a cooler bag, smoked a cigarette and put the butt inside the empty can which he half buried in the sand. He ignored Sandra. I wondered if she had fallen asleep. It was getting late. I figured we would need to head out soon. Maggie always insisted on cleaning all the sand off our feet before getting in the car. I assumed this was something all car owners would care about, so I took my runners and towel and went down to the water. After rinsing off my feet, drying them and putting my runners on, I headed back towards Steve and Sandra. The sun was even lower by now and I noticed the skin on my arms and legs had a different glow from the little bit of tan and the late afternoon light. Steve watched me walk up from the water. Sandra was still wrapped immobile in her towel. Having Steve's eyes on me made me feel strange. I wanted him to notice me, but I was also afraid of him. Afraid of his cut up face, nicotine stained fingers and ropy arms.

"Are we heading home soon?" I stood at the end of Steve's towel. Other groups were starting to gather their belongings.

"I might just have one more beer." Steve reached into the cooler bag, "nothing left in here. I got some more in the car." Sandra shifted slightly in her towel. Steve looked up at me "why don't you come with me to the car to grab another one? When I'm done drinking it, we'll head out."

Sandra lifted her head. "She's not going to the car with you." Steve looked over at her.

"I guess she can come to the car with me if she wants to. It's not up to you." Steve moved his foot so that it was touching mine in the sand. I had my runners on, but his feet were still bare.

Sandra sat up. Her jaw was set and she didn't look at either Steve or me. "She's not going to the car with you." Her voice was quiet, but not shaky. I moved my foot away from Steve's and moved towards Sandra.

Steve didn't say anything. He smoked another cigarette, dropped the butt in the beer can and then stood up to go. Sandra and I followed him silently back to the car. We stayed silent most of the way home. Just north of Steeles the car started making some funny noises and Steve started to swear. Sandra had been looking out of the window, but now she turned her head towards him. Talking almost to herself, she shook her head, "That doesn't sound too good." She smiled. "Maybe we should just grab the bus."

"Yeah, whatever. I'll call my buddy to have a look at it." Steve pulled into a strip mall. Sandra and I walked to the bus stop at the corner. As we stood waiting for the bus, we could see Steve had popped the hood of the Toyota and was standing over it looking frustrated.

"Serves him right, the perv." Sandra said, under her breath. By the time the bus took us to Finch station, Sandra was herself again. Steve was "the perv" from that day forward, although I never really understood why. I did understand that she had saved me from Steve. I was grateful, and I trusted Sandra's guidance on everything, even if my instincts would have led me in the opposite way.

EGG NOG

My instinct was to avoid alcohol. I knew that my bio-parents had been drunks, partiers. That's how I first ended up with Children's Aid. My dad was in jail and my mom had moved to the party house in Stouffville. After being found alone in that field, Children's Aid got involved. Arlene couldn't get her act together too well, but the Children's Aid people tried to help her out and see if she could make it work. That's why I was five before Harold and Maggie took me.

Harold and Maggie had married young and raised three of their own kids. When they were all old enough to be out most of the time, Harold and Maggie didn't like how quiet the house was. They decided to bring me in "to make some noise" is what they told me. I tried to oblige them even though I wasn't a noisy child by nature, they didn't seem to mind. One other thing about Harold and Maggie. They didn't drink.

We were in grade nine. Sandra had gotten a babysitting gig for New Year's Eve. I didn't know the family. Diane and Pete were their names, they had just come from Newfoundland.

They were people her mom knew. The baby was small, and she may have already been asleep by the time we arrived.

Diane and Pete lived in an apartment that was too small for a big Christmas tree, but they had some decorations around. They had strung Christmas lights around the window. There was a small table below the window with a red tablecloth and pine boughs – which I thought was really elegant. I was even more impressed by the cut glass punch bowl with egg nog.

The only egg nog Harold and Maggie had was straight from the Sealtest carton: sweet and cold and slippery. I wasn't sure if I enjoyed it or not. Diane and Pete's egg nog looked totally different.

"It's got rum in it," said Sandra. How she knew this, I don't know. Maybe Diane and Pete had told her. Maybe she had smelled it. Sandra seemed to know all the ins and outs of drinking. One of the tidbits she would share about her dad (long out of the picture) was that he had money.

"He doesn't even need to return his empties when he wants to buy a packet of smokes." I remember her telling me this, and I nodded wisely as if I understood what she was talking about. Eventually I pieced it all together, but it was evidence of Sandra's sophistication and understanding of the way things worked that I was desperate to acquire.

We were there with the boozy egg nog. It was late at night. I was not at home with Harold and Maggie. I could picture them sitting at home, watching TV or reading, or maybe they were in bed already. I was in (what seemed to me) a glamorous apartment with Sandra. We were looking out of the window to see if we could see any fireworks.

"You can drink some. They won't know the difference. They'll be so hammered when they get home." Sandra assumed that I would want to drink some. I didn't want to be the square one who didn't know what "empties" were or how many you needed to return to afford a packet of smokes. I didn't want to say how scared I was to drink, to end up like my bio-parents. I tried to put Harold and Maggie out of my mind and relax into the persona that Sandra seemed to think I could inhabit. An egg nog drinking version of myself, still myself, I reasoned, just a cooler version. Drinking this rum-laced egg nog wouldn't be anything like the drunken parties my bio-parents had, I reasoned to myself. I was a cool thing to do; I knew Sandra would be impressed.

The egg nog tasted terrible. I didn't enjoy it at all, but I had had my first alcoholic drink. I felt amazingly grown up. Sandra was totally nonchalant.

I never drank spiked egg nog after that one time. We didn't get sick or even tipsy really, but I was a person who drank now and sometimes I wonder who I would have become if I had not started that night. It was a few years before I really found the bottle, but that was the first sip, and I took it to impress Sandra. Where she led, I followed.

MARC ANDRE

———— ı|ıı ————

At seventeen, Sandra's friend Alicia from the old neighbourhood on Queen East got pregnant. When the baby was due to be born, Sandra called to tell me about it. "They think it's a boy because her belly is really high and pointy. Raymond says the baby could be his, but Carlo says he's living in a dream world."

I had never met Alicia, or Carlo (or Raymond for that matter) but when Alicia had the baby Sandra assumed I would go with her for the baby's baptism. It was going to be on a Sunday afternoon. I usually would not go out with friends on a Sunday. It was a family day, but Sandra assumed and I didn't want to disappoint her. Needing to spend time with family was too lame of an excuse for not going to Alicia's baby's baptism.

Harold and Maggie were confused. "Who is this Alicia?" Maggie asked.

"She's a good friend of Sandra."

"And how old is she?"

I guessed that seventeen was not going to be a good answer, but I couldn't straight out lie to Maggie, so I just fudged an answer. "She's older. Sandra's mom is going." I wasn't one hundred percent sure of this, but Sandra had mentioned that her mom knew Alicia's mom.

Harold and Maggie looked at one another with worried expressions. I think they wanted to tell me that I couldn't go, but they couldn't find a way to do that without letting me know that Sandra and her mom and all her Queen East friends were low-class trash that I shouldn't be hanging out with. I was offended that they didn't trust me. What did they think, that I would get pregnant by going to a baptism?

I did go to the baptism and that is where I met Marc Andre, who could be called my first boyfriend. Sandra knew Marc Andre mainly because he was friends with Jean Luc. Their families had immigrated from New Brunswick around the same time and they lived close to one another in the Queen East neighbourhood. Although the boys spoke English without accents, having grown up in Toronto, they had these super French names and could speak French fluently. Jean Luc was gorgeous, curly dark hair, ruddy complexion, athletic (he played hockey, of course). Marc Andre was his not gorgeous side kick. In that way Jean Luc and Marc Andre were a mirror image of Sandra and me. Marc Andre was gangly with a cluster of acne on his forehead. His hair was longish, cut in no discernible style. He wore a lumber jacket, jeans and work boots, like scores of other boys you would see slouching aimlessly around Queen East.

Marc Andre had figured out that he was never going to get the really good looking girls, so he didn't even bother with Sandra. He sat next to me at the baptism party. Alicia's mom was hosting the party in her apartment over a hardware store on Queen Street. I was fascinated to see the streetcar going by the living room windows. Marc Andre lived in a very similar apartment two stores down.

"You friends with Sandra?" Marc Andre mumbled while clutching a can of coke.

I wasn't afraid of boys. Harold and Maggie's sons were always around and I knew what boys were like. But I didn't know how to interact with a boy you thought you might like, or a boy you thought might like you. I tried to observe the way the other girls did it, but I couldn't bring myself to flip my hair around and giggle like they did. I felt my cheeks grow hot just thinking about it.

"You want to go up on the roof?" asked Marc Andre. I wasn't sure why I would want to do that, but I sensed that "yes" was the right answer.

"Okay, sure."

Sandra was up there with Jean Luc. They were kissing energetically. I realized this was what "going up to the roof" meant and I had a moment of panic. I couldn't look at Marc Andre. I just let him take my hand and lead me to a sheltered spot on the rooftop, near the door to the stairs.

Even though it was March, the weather was still wintery, and the air was cold on the roof. I didn't have a warm jacket and I was glad to have Marc Andre's warm body come close to me. Like most boys he put out heat like a hot ember. I was happy to put my cold hands inside his lumber jacket. He smelled like a not unpleasant mixture of cigarette smoke and cooked meat.

"Are you shy?" he asked. The tone he used was gentle. I was surprised to hear a boy talking in that tone. It made me feel less nervous. I shook my head. No I was not shy. Marc Andre kissed me.

Strangely, the thing I thought of first was whether Sandra could see me. I wanted her to see me kissing Marc Andre, although we weren't as energetic as she and Jean Luc. She did see us. She took a breath from Jean Luc and looked over at us.

Her expression was conspiratorial. "Look at us, kissing with these French boys," she seemed to say. Although we were both lip-locked with different boys on separate corners of the Queen Street rooftop, the strongest bond that day was between me and Sandra.

We started going down to Queen East regularly, every weekend for sure and sometimes Sandra wanted to go down there after school. I didn't really want to go after school. I didn't mind the rooftop kissing sessions, but I didn't love them either. Besides it was always a grungy ride downtown when all the other schools were letting out and groups of kids from those schools would monopolize buses and subway cars and it was a quick thing to look at someone the wrong way and then we would have a problem. Sandra couldn't move through any environment without attracting attention. She wouldn't go out of her way to look for a confrontation, but if someone rubbed her the wrong way she wouldn't back down. It never got too serious. Some name calling, some pushing, maximum some hair pulling; but I hated that stuff. I just wanted to go about my business peacefully. I would a thousand times rather walk away than get into an argument with someone, but walking away was never going to happen with Sandra.

I wanted to go home after school, do my homework, have dinner with Harold and Maggie, relax in my room listening to music and go to sleep. But Sandra was compelling as always, so 3:15 often found us boarding the Finch bus to start the long trek to Queen East.

Marc Andre almost never spoke. We were always either in a group where others were talking, or we were kissing, which didn't allow for much talking. He never told me that he liked me, he never told me anything about his interests or his family, and then one day:

"Are we going to get married?" Marc Andre whispered during a pause in our kissing. He spoke quietly, but I was absolutely certain of the words. I felt dizzy. What was he saying? We barely knew one another. I was pretty sure he didn't like me very much, and I was sure I didn't have any kind of feelings of the sort that would lead to marriage. I imagined what that could look like: me married to Marc Andre. Would I hang out with Alicia and the baby? Would we live in one of the apartments above the stores on Queen Street? Would we quit school? It was a strange vision of a future totally unlike anything I had imagined for myself up to that point.

I don't think I said anything to Marc Andre. The whole thing was so fantastical, I didn't even tell Sandra. I guess it was too embarrassing or just too strange. But a part of me felt mysterious and glamorous.

That mystery and glamour faded quickly the following week when I got a call from Cody. "This is Cody. I'm a friend of Marc Andre," he announced when I answered the phone.

"Yeah. Okay."

"Yeah. Marc Andre wants me to tell you that you're dumped." And that was the end of my first relationship. I knew that I was supposed to feel sad, or heartbroken, or angry maybe. I did feel a little sad. My ego was hurt by the brutality of the "you're dumped" phone call, but the primary emotion I felt was relief.

We didn't go down to Queen East anymore. Sandra and Jean Luc stayed together, but he would come up to our neighbourhood until he said it was too far to come on the bus, and they broke up too.

BIOLOGICAL PARENTS

"So Harold and Maggie aren't your real parents?" The question hung in the air for a minute. I wasn't ashamed to say that I was adopted. Harold and Maggie had always been super open about it. But I was nervous about telling Sandra because I didn't want anything to make me less worthy to be her friend.

We had been sitting in my bedroom doing math homework when Sandra explained, "My mom says we Kerrys are not good at math, it's not in our genes." Math was okay for me. I liked the predictability and the certainty of a correct answer. "Harold's an engineer, that's why you're good at math. You must have got it from him." Sandra was pleased with herself for coming up with this explanation. She felt justified in copying my answers for the homework given the genetic lottery situation.

The idea of inheriting any traits from Harold made me feel so strange that I had to set her straight, "I didn't get it from Harold. I'm adopted."

Sandra processed this information for a minute and looked at me, "so Harold and Maggie aren't your real parents?"

"No"

"Huh. I never would have guessed." She went back to copying my answers and we didn't talk about it again until the day the Children's Aid worker was sitting with Maggie at the dining room table when I got home from school.

Even after I went to live with Harold and Maggie, my bio-mom still had chances to see me. When I was seven, when I was nine, twice when I was ten. Each of those times there would be a build up: Harold and Maggie would talk to me and reassure me that they were still my parents, that nothing would change that. The day of the visit would approach and I would start getting stomach aches and having nightmares. I felt bad for being scared. I wanted to want to see my bio-mom, but the mental picture I had of her was hard to square with the idea of "mother". I could remember the smell of alcohol and cigarettes, I could remember a young woman with a thin face laughing at some video she was watching. I could remember the flashing lights of a police car. Cold air that went right through the thin material of my pyjamas as the police officer took me out of the house and into a waiting social worker's car. The sound of my bio-mom crying and cursing the cop.

She never turned up at any of those planned visits. Sometimes there was an explanation provided, sometimes the exhausted social worker would just say, "Well, I guess she's not coming. Let's get you home Frida."

I was fourteen when the Children's Aid showed up that day at the dining room table. I couldn't believe that my bio-mom was trying for another visit after all this time.

"Hi Frida, this is Joanne from Children's Aid." Maggie telegraphed me a reassuring look. Maybe there was no visit. So what did they want?

"Maggie tells me you've started high school! That's so exciting!" Joanne was nervous. She was young and pretty. She wore a nice blue and green scarf. I had a feeling that something was up. The CAS workers I knew were usually more battle worn. Why did they send me this fresh one?

"Frida, I'm here today because I need to tell you something about your mom, Arlene." Joanne reached across the table as though she wanted to touch me. I stiffened and moved back in my chair so that she would not be able to. She left her arm on the table with her hand turned up towards me. "Unfortunately, Frida, we have been informed that your biological mother died in Vancouver last month."

I was not expecting that.

Joanne and her scarf left pretty quickly. Maggie took her card and said we would call her in a couple of days. I went up to my room and sent a message to Sandra:

need to talk can u come over?
on my way

While waiting for Sandra to arrive I tried to rehearse how I would give her the news. "Turns out my bio-mom is dead," is what I decided I would go with. I wondered if I should try to cry. Then I wondered whether it was weird that I should have to try to cry. Shouldn't I just cry because I was sad? Because my mom was dead?

Maggie told Sandra when she let her in the house, so I didn't need to deliver my rehearsed line after all. As soon as Sandra came into my room and I saw her face, the tears came. And I didn't have to try.

"Shit, Frida. I'm so sorry. It's terrible." Sandra dropped her bag at the foot of my bed, sat beside me and put her arms around me. We both just cried and hung on to one another. It felt good and terrible at the same time. It was like a wound at the centre of my chest had been opened up, but the tears and Sandra's strong arms around me made the ache of that wound bearable.

"What happened? Did they say how she died?" Sandra finally asked when we had run out of crying energy.

"She had moved to Vancouver, they said, and was living in a really rough neighbourhood. The social worker said that she died of an overdose." My understanding of what overdosing meant was pretty weak. Joanne had been vague with the details.

"Oh shit." Sandra didn't ask anything more about that. She switched gears, "Frida. What about your real dad? Do you even know him?"

I had never given much thought to my bio-dad. The only information I had about him I had overheard when two social workers were talking while I had been waiting for my mom to show up for one of the visits that never happened. I had gone to the bathroom. I guess they thought I was still in the sitting room they had for people to wait in. They were drinking coffee in a little kitchenette off the hallway that joined the sitting room and the bathroom.

Social worker #1: "Such a shame. Why does she set up these visits if she's not going to show? The poor kid!"

Social worker #2: "I know. It would be better for her if Arlene would just leave her alone."

Social worker #1: "What about the father? Is he in the picture?

Social worker #2: "The only thing Arlene ever said about him was that he worked up north in mining or something. He stayed with Arlene and Frida for a year, but then he went to jail and Arlene went to Stouffville. When he came out of jail, Arlene just said that 'he fucked off back up north'. He hasn't been heard from since."

I didn't want to tell Sandra that all I knew about my dad was that he had been in jail and that he worked up north "in mining or something".

I hugged my pillow shaped like the letter 'F' for Frida that Maggie had given me for my thirteenth birthday, "No I don't know him."

"Well, if he's anything like my dad that's not much of a loss. Whenever I go over there Annemarie, his girlfriend, gives me a hard time. She wants me to do dishes and yard work and shit. Can you believe that? Like what has Kieran Kelly ever done for me? He got me one lousy Christmas gift in the past five years. It was a stupid shirt that was way too small for me. My mom says he's a no good ....."

Sandra's tirade about her dad gave me a chance to tune out. I went into a kind of sleep mode while she rambled on. Eventually I did actually fall asleep. I heard her get up to leave, but I pretended to be deeply asleep so I didn't have to say anything more. That night I dreamed about my bio-mom being trapped in a deep mine shaft surrounded by pill bottles and glasses of wine. I was looking down into the shaft and trying to think of how I could get a rope down to her. A man wearing a baseball cap with some kind of logo on it was there with me, looking down into the mine. He didn't speak. He just looked sad.

Maggie called Joanne a couple of days later. We were in the kitchen and Maggie put the phone on speaker so I could hear what Joanne had to say. Maggie wanted to know why it had taken so long for us to be notified about Arlene's death.

"It took the police a while to figure out who the next of kin were because Arlene didn't have any ID on her when they found her. Turns out she had been sharing an apartment with some people, but they said that she often disappeared for days at a time, so when she didn't come home for a few days, they weren't that worried. The police had an idea that she might have been living in the Downtown East Side neighbourhood, so they started asking around and showing her picture. That's when the roommates figured out that Arlene wasn't coming home." Maggie put her arm around my shoulder and I put my head on her chest. I wasn't sure that I could listen to much more, but I just closed my eyes and sort of muffled the sound of Joanne's voice by pressing one ear into Maggie. "The police went to the apartment to see if they could find information about Arlene and who her family was. They found an envelope with some documents including papers about Frida's adoption. That's how they knew to contact us. There's some clothes and there's some pictures that were in the envelope that Frida might want to have."

Maggie thanked Joanne and hung up the phone. We cried there in the kitchen for a long time. The initial shock lasted for a few days and then receded to a tender spot in the centre of my chest that would ache on Mother's Day and other random times. I turned fifteen. I kept going to school and Sandra was always there to give life and meaning to everything I did.

BOUILLABAISSE

We were almost finished grade ten, and Sandra's big idea was that we should get jobs. We went to get our SIN cards and checked the youth employment website, but jobs that we thought we could do were not that easy to come by. Then we met Bruce.

Bruce was in grade twelve, but he wasn't too full of himself to talk to the younger kids. Sandra made friends with him while waiting for the bus. He asked her for a cigarette and they started talking. Bruce had a job in a restaurant. He had already been working there for a few months and he knew people who worked as dishwashers, busboys, even waiters. He was a busboy, but was close to being promoted to waiter.

"It's perfect, if you both come in they'll have all the bussers they need and I'll be promoted. They're short one waiter since Armand got fired for stealing booze." Bruce spoke quickly and with self assurance. We were in awe. "Come down with me on Thursday and I'll introduce you to Phillipe. He's the owner."

Bouillabaisse was in Yorkville. A small space on Scollard Avenue. It was one of those row houses that held hippie nightclubs in the sixties and now had overpriced boutiques and restaurants like Bouillabaisse. Phillipe was a high strung gay man who dressed impeccably, with a small scarf at his neck that did an almost perfect job of hiding the slightly sagging skin there.

I was fascinated by Phillipe's rings. He wore rings on both hands, some with stones, some without. His hands were thin and sinewy with several scars from burns and cuts earned in his years in the kitchen. Bruce told us that he didn't cook now, he was the owner and host. Occasionally he would pour a glass of wine for a table that deserved extra attention.

Sandra and I were totally out of our element. Before going in, Bruce gave us a once over. He himself had quickly transformed from nondescript suburban high school student to polished Yorkville restaurant employee. He had taken his black backpack and gone into the bathroom at Bloor station (a thing I never would have dared to do), and he came out wearing black shoes, black pants and a white dress shirt. He had wet and combed back his hair and, I couldn't be sure, but maybe he had put on some eyeliner.

Sandra and I did not have a black backpack containing the polish we would need, and Bruce sighed when he looked at us. Long hair (somewhat messy), unfashionable jeans (bought at Bluenotes), running shoes and t-shirts.

"There's nothing we can do about the clothes, but at least tie back your hair."

Sandra was beautiful even with her messy hair and crummy clothes, but then she tied back her hair and put on some lipstick she had stolen from her mom. She ducked into the alleyway beside the restaurant and turned her t-shirt inside out so that the "St. Margaret's Summer Camp for Girls" logo was no longer visible. She looked like a model. I was incredulous. I couldn't bear to check my pale face in the little mirror I carried around with me, I knew I wouldn't look anywhere near as good as Sandra.

We went in. Bouillabaisse had only a small staff. It was just past 4:30, so the waiters and busboys hadn't arrived yet. The kitchen was busy and they had loud music playing, nothing I recognized, it was in French, I thought. Not like the old-fashioned "French cafe" music Madame Fornier played in French class at school, more like the kind of music we would listen to, but in French.

Phillipe had a tiny office downstairs. There was a desk piled high with paper: receipts, invoices, menus, newspapers, magazines. Several dirty dishes and a wine glass were crowded on a small table besides a couch that was against the wall opposite the desk. There was no place to sit aside from Phillipe's chair behind the desk and the couch. It didn't seem right to sit on the couch with those plates and wine glass. Also the couch had the distinct look of a place where someone slept, maybe not every night, but regularly. There was a blanket draped over the back and the cushions held a body-shaped impression.

We stood. Bruce, Sandra and I: three kids from the suburbs crowded into this tiny office. Phillipe was not unkind. He looked Sandra and I up and down without subtlety. After looking at Sandra, he nodded. After looking at me, he raised an eyebrow and looked at Bruce. Bruce smiled and shrugged his shoulders. I moved closer to Sandra to make it clear we were a package deal.

Phillipe took a drag of his cigarette and rested the butt on a tiny brass ashtray. "You can start tomorrow. You'll need black pants or skirt, black shoes and a white shirt. Make sure your hair is tied back, and no nail polish."

We were set! We had jobs! We had no idea what was in store for us. There were three waiters (four, if you included newly promoted Bruce), but they never spoke to us. We got our orders from Tomasz, the head busboy, a Polish immigrant who I estimated was in his early twenties. He explained everything to us on our first shift. First job was to learn how to set the table correctly, including how to line up the water glass with the knife and how to measure how far from the edge of the table the cutlery had to sit: one thumbnail. It was a lot to take in, but we paid attention and watched Tomasz as if our lives depended on it.

Bruce had told us, "When you're working, just focus on the job you are doing. Don't think about the boy at school you have a crush on, don't think about homework or what movie you're going to see on the weekend. Just pay attention to what you are doing." This may have been the best piece of advice anyone had ever given me.

It was difficult job because in addition to all the rules about setting the tables, there were the rules about clearing the tables. "Clear from the left, pick up the plates and then use the cutlery to push any leftover food onto one plate you hold in your hand. The others you balance in a stack on your forearm," Tomasz explained. And when he did it, it looked easy. Those plates were heavy, and my forearms were stick thin and not strong enough to carry more than two plates at a time.

Then there was the coffee. Part of our job was to make the coffees using the huge Italian espresso machine at the bar. Tomasz explained how to clear the used coffee grounds from the portafilter with a sharp bang on the garbage container that was solely for used grounds, then fill the portafilter from the coffee grinder. "Always double check that the grinder has enough coffee in it. Tamp down the coffee and attach the portafilter to the machine with a firm twist. If it's not properly attached boiling hot water will spray into your face. Switch on for the coffee to flow into the little espresso cups." So far, so good if the customer had ordered espresso. But many customers wanted cappuccino, which required steamed milk. "The milk has to be cold. Put the steam wand into the flask, heat the milk first, and then slowly, gently bring the nozzle to the top to make the foam." Easier said than done. We learned, but the steaming, gleaming espresso machine featured prominently in my anxiety dreams for weeks.

STRAWBERRIES

Sandra and I were together almost all the time. We would always be together at school, we were in almost all the same classes, then on Thursday through Sunday we would ride together down to Yorkville to work at Bouillabaisse until eleven or twelve o'clock at night. Then we would ride back to North York together.

Maggie and Harold were happy I had a job. School was almost finished and I would have a job for the summer now. They were firm believers in the values of hard work and self sufficiency. They never came to Bouillabaisse, in fact Harold couldn't pronounce Bouillabaisse. The only restaurants I remember going to with Harold and Maggie were Swiss Chalet and one Chinese place on Finch. Harold and Maggie still weren't sure about Sandra, but they realized that she was the most important person in my life. I only had a vague idea of myself apart from Sandra, but that was about to change. I can say exactly when. It was one weekend in June of grade ten. That one weekend Sandra and I didn't work together. That weekend I made an important discovery and Sandra met Carly.

Harold's brother and his wife had come up from the States to visit, so I took the weekend off. Harold's brother Frank was younger than him and much more free-spirited. He played the guitar and his wife Eileen was a yoga instructor and believer in crystals and psychic energy. Frank and Eileen were fun to be around and they teased Harold the whole weekend.

Harold and I had always been a bit stand-offish with one another. He had exhausted most of his parenting energy with his own three boys and was a little unsure of what to do with this pale, skinny girl Maggie had convinced him to adopt. He was an engineer and saw the world through a fairly narrow lens. He was closed-minded, but in a sort of benign way. Other ideas or visions of the world were just confusing and he didn't want to bother trying to figure them out.

Frank seemed to revel in poking fun at his staid older brother. "You should let Eileen do a reading for you Harold. It would be good for you to understand why your energies are so blocked."

Harold was like a deer caught in headlights. I could see his mind trying to put together the meaning of what Frank had said. He must have thought Frank was suggesting Eileen read the hydro meter. Harold knew that Eileen was a yoga instructor, and not trained to read a hydro meter, so that must be wrong. There was no energy blockage, as far as he knew, so he didn't really know what to say. Harold was never rude, so he just mumbled something like, "yes, very good idea," and nodded nervously. Eileen and Frank burst out laughing.

Eileen took pity on him. "Don't worry, Harold. Frank is teasing you. Your energy is just fine." Harold looked relieved. It was unsettling, but exciting, to see Harold in this light. Someone who could be caught in an uncomfortable situation. Some who could be made fun of.

Eileen was a bird lover, so we decided to go down to the Leslie Street Spit where there were apparently lots of birds to be seen. It was strange to be near Marc Andre and Jean Luc's neighbourhood again. It felt like a lifetime had passed since those rooftop kissing sessions, but it had only been a year. Sitting in the back of Harold and Maggie's car driving along Queen Street gave me a bizarre, almost out of body sensation. I felt like if I looked out the window of the car I might see myself and Sandra walking there. But no. I was me. In the back seat of Harold and Maggie's car, squeezed between Frank and Eileen.

We walked for a while on the Spit. It was a beautiful day and lots of people were out walking and biking. Eileen got pretty excited about the cormorants.

On the way back to the car we walked up Leslie Street and I noticed a weird sort of park. I call it a park, but it was more overgrown, and with lots of fences, so not like a ravine. I was intrigued, so I went over to have a closer look.

A chain-link fence ran along the length of the property, but beyond the perimeter fence, inside the enclosure, I could see there were more fences of various types which divided the property into dozens of plots, each one the size of a really big bed, or two beds side by side. There was all kinds of stuff growing in the various plots: flowers, vegetables, vines, fruit. There were people in quite a few of the plots, watering, weeding, digging. I couldn't really understand what it all meant. It was obviously not an organized farm, but it also was not one person's garden.

I must have looked really perplexed. A dark-skinned guy a few years older than me spoke to me from the other side of the fence, "you looking for someone?"

"What is this place?" I asked.

He smiled and took his hat off to wipe his forehead. His arms and hands were covered with soil and bits of leaves. He didn't look like a muscle-head, but I could see that he was someone used to working with his hands. He was wearing jeans that also had a fair bit of soil on them, and in his pocket he had a red and white cloth which he took out and used to wipe his face. His movements were calm without being slow and he stood with absolute self possession as he spoke to me. "These are allotment gardens," he explained. "Different people take care of each plot. You can grow all kinds of great stuff. Here, try these." He reached down to a low bush that was growing along the edge of what I assumed was his plot, just a little ways in from the outer fence. He gave me a handful of small strawberries over the fence.

"You grew these?"

"Me and my mom. We tend this plot together." There was something different about the way he spoke. Not an accent exactly, but a lilt or a rhythm that was pleasant. I got the impression that he thought about his words before he said them. I put all the strawberries in my mouth at once. They were delicious, sweet, but with a tart freshness that I had never experienced before.

"Those are amazing," I said when I had swallowed. Maggie called to me from further up the road. I could see them standing waiting for me: Harold, Maggie, Frank and Eileen.

"I guess that's your family," strawberry boy said.

"I gotta go. Thanks for the berries." I walked up towards the others. I stayed close to the fence as I walked so I could look in and see the garden plots with all their weird and unmatched crops. Some plots were immaculately kept, with straight rows and upright fences. Others were riots of tangled vegetation enclosed by ramshackle wooden slats. A few had lawn chairs. I was entranced. I decided that I needed a plan to come back here.

We got back in the car. I was tired from walking in the sun, but I felt calm and happy. I thought, as we drove back past Queen Street, that I couldn't wait to tell Sandra about the allotment gardens and the strawberry boy. I didn't know about Carly yet.

CARLY

—— I|I| ——

The next few days at school I barely had a chance to speak to Sandra. Reports cards were coming up and the teachers were going all out with tests and assignments due. We all picked up the vibe and buried our heads in our work, or at least pretended to. Whenever I looked at Sandra, she was looking at her phone. I wondered who she was texting. Strange.

Even stranger, Thursday came and we had a shift together at Bouillabaisse, but when it was time to beeline from school and catch the bus, she was nowhere to be found. I sent a text:

where ru?
left early cu there

When I arrived at Bouillabaisse I went to the locker room to change. No sign of Sandra. Just as I was brushing my hair to put it up, she arrived. But she wasn't alone. She was with Carly. The two of them came into the locker room laughing. At first glance, I thought Carly was the same age as me and Sandra, but then when I looked at her again, she looked younger. She had curly strawberry blonde hair and freckles. Her face was very expressive. It was fascinating to watch her eyes and mouth react to Sandra telling a story about a run-in she had had with one of the waiters. And then she spoke. Now I had to change my opinion again about how old she was because her voice was raspy, like a dedicated smoker, and she swore like the prep cooks. I got a bad vibe from her right away, but Sandra seemed to be right into her.

They were laughing so much, I felt a little awkward. I obviously wasn't in on the joke. Tomasz came into the locker room. He looked at Sandra and Carly, then he put his bag in his locker and proceeded to comb his already immaculately coiffed hair.

"You better not let Philippe see you two high like that."

This just made Sandra and Carly laugh even more. I was confused and embarrassed. All I could think to do was to go into automatic pilot. Set the tables, fill the bread baskets, get ready for the first tables. I was glad it was a busy night although I ended up run off my feet since Carly and I were working the same section and she was useless. I had done all the table settings by the time she came out of the locker room. She would only clear half the dirty dishes off a table, then she would start chatting with the dishwasher or checking her phone.

About forty minutes into our shift she told me, "I'm going to grab a smoke." I didn't say anything, just kept on doing the work of two people as best I could.

Twenty minutes later Tomasz asked me, "Where's Carly?"

"She went for a smoke." He could see my frustration, and without another word, he cleared three tables, made four cappuccinos and when out back to drag Carly back to work. She didn't even look guilty when she came back. I couldn't imagine being told off by Tomasz. Just a glance from him was enough to make me scurry off to find work that needed to be done.

At the end of the night, Carly parked herself at the bar with the waiters and ordered a beer. Sandra and I left. It was a school day the next day. As we walked to Bay station I thought about telling Sandra about the allotment gardens and the strawberry boy, but she was full of stories about the weekend shifts with Carly and "who did Tomasz think he was, ordering us all around?" I decided that I would tell her another time.

I had learned to be a better cigarette smoker since the early days when Sandra first taught me, but I didn't like to smoke at work. In the dining room, the smell of a restaurant is pleasant: the food, the perfume and cologne of the diners out for a nice evening, but once you leave the dining room and go near the kitchen the smells are more intense. The raw ingredients: garlic, fish, meat, spices have not yet been magically combined, and their individual aromas hit you together with the smell of hot oil, and the heat and smoke from the cooktops and ovens. Even stronger smells would emanate from the dishpit where two dishwashers worked in a fetid steam bath of uneaten food, dirty dishes, cups and glasses, scraps and dirty pans from the kitchen all mixed with the smell of industrial strength detergent and bleach. I couldn't bear the idea of adding the smell of cigarette smoke to all that.

Carly and Sandra would go out two, three times per shift, always trying to evade Tomasz's surveillance. Sandra ditched me on Thursday and Friday of the following week. She skipped last period and went down to Yorkville to meet up with Carly and get high. I didn't say anything to Sandra about it.

Saturday nights were always the busiest. We wouldn't be finished until at least midnight, and usually Sandra and I just hobbled home to rest up when we were done. This Saturday after we finished our shift, I went to the locker room and changed out of my work shirt. I took my hair down and put on lipstick.

"Why are you getting all dolled up?" asked Sandra "Aren't we going home?"

"In a bit," I said. I felt nervous playing this part, since it was always Sandra who decided what we were going to do and when.

We left the locker room and instead of heading out the door, I went to the bar where the waiters were sitting. Tomasz was behind the bar, and Carly was there. I knew a lot depended on how I behaved. One wrong move or word and I would be laughed back to North York.

I spotted an empty stool next to Bruce and I went straight for it. I launched into animated chit chat with Bruce about mutual friends. I played it super cool. I didn't look at Carly; I was sure that Sandra had gone to sit with her.

I could feel Tomasz looking at me, but I didn't dare return his gaze. I knew I would lose my nerve. "Bruce, you want another one?" asked Tomasz, taking away Bruce's empty beer bottle.

"Sure, same again, Tomasz. Thanks."

I cleared my throat. Bruce looked at me. "You want one?" he asked. Of course at that precise moment, everyone else stopped talking, the song that had been playing came to an end, even the eternal noise of the kitchen crew doing their clean up seemed to pause. Tomasz got a beer for Bruce and closed the fridge. He looked at me expectantly.

"I'll have a Heineken, thanks, Tomasz," I said breezily (at least I hoped it sounded breezy). How did I decide that I should order a Heineken? Nobody else at the bar was drinking Heineken. It wasn't a popular beer at the restaurant, the customers drank mostly wine anyway. I knew about Heineken because Frank and Eileen had brought some when they came for their visit. Even Harold had some. The bottles were a distinctive green and when Frank brought them out I had noticed them and remembered the name. I was pretty sure I had never seen that type of bear bottle before. It had not been amongst the bottles and cans and glasses on the coffee table at the party house in Stouffville.

Tomasz smiled, "Okay, Frida. Heineken it is. You earned it tonight." He went to the fridge and pulled out the distinctive green bottle. I was determined to drink that beer and sit at that bar and show Carly and Sandra that I was just as cool as them.

I sat beside Bruce. I drank my Heineken and listened to Tomasz tell stories about Poland. It was almost one o'clock in the morning when everyone started to get up to leave. Sandra and Carly had gone out to smoke and now they were back. Carly saw my Heineken bottle. "You like that stuff? Ew. It tastes like piss," she said with a sneer.

"Shut up, Carly," said Tomasz, "you know nothing." Carly stood with her mouth open for half a second. I could see the colour rising around her hairline.

"You shut up, Tomasz!" was all she could come up with as a come back. Sandra and Carly took their bags and left.

On the way out, Sandra called to me, "Bye, Frida! Text you tomorrow."

Bruce and I rode home to North York together. I nodded off as the subway swayed us gently up Yonge Street. Bruce nudged me awake when we got to Finch. "End of the line, Frida. Time to get off."

MICHAL

School finished and we picked up more hours at Bouillabaisse. They had a small patio where they could serve lunch in the nice weather. This was a popular spot; customers would eat their pasta and salads and drink rosé wine. Business was so good, even Philippe smiled sometimes.

I still couldn't stand Carly and it bothered me that Sandra would go off with her to smoke or whatever, but there was nothing I could do about it and I figured Carly wouldn't last long at Bouillabaisse since she was the absolute worst at her job.

When I wasn't working at Bouillabaisse I started going down to the allotment gardens. Sandra's reaction when I told her about it had been muted, "A bunch of gardens? Near Ashbridges Bay? Doesn't it smell like sewer down there?" She barely looked up from her phone. I was disappointed that she didn't seem to be interested. I imagined us going down there together on the Queen car just like in the old days, except instead of going to see Marc Andre and Jean Luc, we would go and work in the garden. I didn't tell her about strawberry boy, because she would think it was lame that I hadn't gotten his phone number or even found out his name. I thought I would go and see him again and try to get to know him so that could be a draw for Sandra to come with me.

Not just anyone can get access to the allotment gardens. You're only supposed to go in if you have a plot. But the gardeners were a little cult-like and if they saw an outsider who looked like a potential convert, they would start talking to you and invite you in. That's how I got to meet a bunch of people: Carol, an old lady with long white hair who grew zinnias and daisies; Giuseppe, an Italian TTC operator who grew tomatoes; Cecilia, a tiny Chinese woman who grew all kinds of vegetables that I didn't know the names of; and, of course, Lionel (aka strawberry boy) who had been the first one to talk to me over the fence.

Lionel, I learned, was studying at George Brown college and working part time at a sports equipment store. He said that he didn't like the job, but he needed the money. I told him about my job, but we were preparing a portion of his plot for planting peppers at the time, so I didn't go into too much detail. Lionel was keen on explaining to me how you needed to feed the soil in order to grow good crops.

"We already had spinach and radishes out of this bed this year, so we can't expect peppers to grow without putting something in." There was a free pile of compost near the entrance to the garden. I had already been given the sermon on the importance of composting and how valuable a material it was, so I went and filled a wheelbarrow with the "magic material" and Lionel and I dug it into the bed.

*   *   *

Tomasz was the one who explained to me why Carly hadn't been fired. I came in grim-faced one day because I was scheduled to work with her. "Why you make that face like you just eat a lemon, Frida?"

"It's not fair that I have to pick up her slack."

Tomasz was cleaning the espresso machine. He loved that thing and kept it gleaming. He would check the water pressure gauge like a mother checking a child's temperature. "Nobody cares, Frida. Just do your job. Yes, Carly is shit at bussing tables, but she has right look and Philippe knows customers don't come here just for the food."

I knew that asking him what they came for, if not for the food, would have revealed, once again, my ignorance and inexperience, so I just nodded and went to work.

That day I watched Carly more closely. It was hard for me to acknowledge, despising her as I did, but she was attractive. She had those freckles that made her look so innocent, but she moved in a way that made it look as though her clothes were just about to fall off of their own accord and when she spoke it was always dirty. She was fascinating.

I realized that there were a few regular customers who would come and sit on the patio and talk to Carly. All men. All with expensive watches and fancy shoes. One guy in particular would come almost every day. If Carly was working he would hang around drinking coffee and talking to her when she was supposed to be working. His name, Tomasz told me, was Michal.

"See, he parks his BMW on Scollard even though he gets ticket every day."

Incredibly, not only did Philippe not fire Carly, he promoted her to waiting tables. It was hard to keep wait staff during the summer; Yorkville's patios were in constant competition for staff as well as customers. Philippe promoted Tomasz too, but not to waiter, his accent was too thick, especially for the American tourists. Tomasz was now the bartender. As a waitress, Carly had even more reason to chat and flirt with Michal and the other flashy Yorkville crowd.

I thought I would try to chat up the customers like Carly, but the flashy ones just looked right through me. I had moderate success with one old guy who turned out to be a university professor. He only ever ordered a salad and drank water, so Philippe told me, "Just clear his table as soon as he's finished. If we can get him out quickly we can seat someone else who will order a cocktail or a dessert at least."

Sandra was working mainly evenings, so more than a week had gone by since we last worked together. It was Saturday night in July. Bouillabaisse was hopping. Carly and Bruce were waiting tables, Tomasz was behind the bar and Sandra and I were bussing. Philippe had to help out, especially since Sandra was just as bad at waiting tables as she had been at bussing. I recognized several of the lunchtime regulars, including Michal, at a big table. It was different from lunchtime because now they had women with them.

Michal's table was ordering full meals and lots of drinks. They started getting loud right after the appetizers, and by the time dessert came Michal and the other two guys at the table were drunk and talking animatedly in their language. The women went to the bathroom at least four times during the meal, and since the men at their table weren't paying any attention to them, they moved to the bar.

Tomasz's job as bartender was obviously to make the drinks, but he also controlled the sound system. Generally the music at Bouillabaisse was jazz or some French music, but that night the women sweet-talked Tomasz into playing some music they had on their phones. They started singing along and then dancing in the narrow space in front of the bar.

It was crazy. Bruce and Carly were having trouble hearing the orders from customers because Michal and his friends were yelling, the music was loud and the women were singing at the top of their lungs. Sandra and I had to weave around the dancers when clearing tables because the area they had turned into a dance floor was between the dining room and the kitchen.

For once the noise in the dining room was louder than the kitchen. Francois, the cook, stepped out in his whites to see what was going on. Michal summoned him over, "Francois! You're a genius! Come and drink whiskey with us!" Francois was tired, having been in the kitchen since ten that morning. I could see that the last thing he wanted to was to drink whiskey with these guys, but he caught Philippe's eye and said,

"Well, thanks Michal. Just one."

The other tables left. At midnight Philippe told Sandra and me to go home. Michal's table was still going. The women had stopped singing and dancing, but they were now draped over Michal's friends kissing them and whispering in their ears. Michal wasn't at the table. I figured he must be in the bathroom.

Sandra and I went to the locker room. We were too exhausted to speak. My head was pounding, Sandra said that she had a blister on one heel. We left by the kitchen door and started south on the narrow laneway that ran alongside the building, connecting Scollard to Yorkville Avenue. There was usually a light in this laneway, but it had burned out earlier that week and Philippe had not had a chance to replace it.

We were walking slowly down the laneway when Sandra stopped suddenly and put her hand on my arm to stop me. She gestured ahead. When I looked where she had pointed, I could see two people making out in a doorway. It was pretty dark in the laneway, but there was no mistaking who those two people were. The man had his hand up the woman's skirt and her shirt was half off, revealing a bare shoulder and bra. It was Michal and Carly.

Without saying anything, Sandra and I walked back up the laneway towards Scollard. Michal and Carly hadn't seen us.

AMIR

———— ı|ı| ————

Bouillabaisse changed after that night. Not all at once, but by mid-August it was like a different place. The older ladies who used to come for lunch didn't come anymore. Michal and his friends took over. They seemed to always be there and they behaved as if they owned the place. They would go behind the bar and change the music. They brought their own liquor which they would drink late into the night. One day I heard Philippe and Francois yelling at one another in French. Tomasz told me they were fighting because Michal had asked Philippe to add a traditional Albanian dish to the menu.

"Francois is insulted. 'I trained at the Cordon Bleu'" Tomasz did a great imitation of Francois, "'I am a French chef! I do not cook mama's lamb stew from the old country!'" We laughed at the idea of Michal giving Francois pointers on cooking.

Carly and Michal would often be seen getting hot and heavy in the alleyway or sometimes even inside the restaurant or in the bathrooms. He would pull her onto his lap when she came to take the orders. She would pretend to be mad and all the guys at the table would laugh.

Sandra and I watched Carly with amazement. At the end of one long night, we saw her get into Michal's sleek black car. He held the door open for her and she laughed and tossed her hair like a movie star as she got into the car.

"That's a nice car," Sandra was looking at her phone to see if we had missed the last subway north.

"He's so old. Why does she go with him?"

Sandra shrugged, "He's rich. He buys her things." This was true. The longer things went on with Michal, the more Carly transformed. First she got acrylic nails that would clatter annoyingly on the order screen by the bar. I could see it set Tomasz's teeth on edge. Then she got a new designer bag. She wouldn't leave it in the locker room where Sandra and I left our things. Philippe had to lock it in the office. One day the discussion was about shoes.

"They have them at Holt's," Carly was perched on a stool at the bar scrolling through images of shoes that cost more than what we would make in a month. Michal was at a table talking on the phone in his language while two other guys sat drinking whiskey. One of these was slightly younger than Michal. He had started coming along with the group in the past few days, but he didn't fit in somehow. He sat apart from the group when they got too loud. He didn't laugh when Michal would slap Carly's bottom or tickle her when she was trying to serve drinks. His clothes didn't seem as slick and I thought I saw a book tucked in the pocket of his jacket.

I had seen him having a friendly argument with Michal about who was going to pay the bill. This was common in the restaurant and servers learned to read the power dynamics so that the bill ended up with the right person. Michal was clearly the top dog in this fight, but the younger guy put on a good show of trying to pay. He left the table and approached Tomasz at the bar to try and pay before the bill even was presented at the table. Michal spotted him.

"No, Amir! You don't pay! Tomasz, do not accept his money." There was some laughing and Amir went to take out his wallet, but it was clear to everyone that Amir was out of his league and this was just for him to save face.

I was making cappuccinos. I had gotten to be an expert at them by now. Even Tomasz didn't feel the need to watch over me as I worked the steam nozzle. But someone was watching me that day. I carefully poured the hot milk into the coffee and layered the foam with a swift, smooth motion that had become unconscious. I added the little sugar bowl to the tray with the coffee cups and prepared to take the tray to the table. When I lifted my head, I could see that Amir was looking at me. It was obvious from his face that he had been watching me the whole time. He smiled and gave an approving nod towards the cappuccinos. "Very beautiful."

I didn't speak. I just blushed and willed myself to carry that tray of coffees carefully to the table. I could feel Amir's eyes follow me as I walked across the restaurant. After serving the coffee, I looked back towards the bar. Amir was not standing there anymore. He was back at the table with Michal and they were talking with their heads close together. Amir kept his eyes on the table and fiddled with a ring on his right hand as Michal spoke to him.

For the next few days I had visions of myself with acrylic nails, designer bags and expensive shoes getting in and out of luxury automobiles. I practised tossing my hair and laughing, but I gave up on that because I felt like a fool. I asked Maggie if I could borrow one of her large carry-all bags. It wasn't designer, but at least it wasn't a backpack with a frayed strap.

Sandra and I had the lunchtime shift on Saturday. I didn't know if Amir would be there, but I washed and straightened my hair and rehearsed clever conversation starters based on the nothing I knew about him.

Sandra said that she would meet me there, so I made my way to Yorkville by myself. I got off at Bay station and walked up towards the restaurant. The streets were busy; people were out walking their dogs. Elegant women walked by with bags from Bloor Street boutiques. I tried to stand up straight and walk like Sandra, but I was acutely aware of how everything about me was wrong. I was like someone who had wandered onto the set of a movie. All the actors moved fluidly in their roles while I stuck out as hopelessly out of place. I could imagine the director calling "Cut!" and having me escorted off the set, back to North York.

As I turned onto Scollard, I could see there was someone already sitting on Bouillabaisse's patio. When I got close enough I could see that it was Amir. He was alone. He was reading a book – the one I had seen in his pocket, I assumed.

I tried to slow my breathing. I combed out my hair with my fingers and searched in Maggie's bag for a mirror to check my face. When I looked up again, Amir was no longer alone. Someone in a black skirt and white shirt was standing by his table. I recognized who it was. She had her tray propped against her hip and she fiddled with the thin gold chain she wore around her neck. He looked up at her with a smile on his face, the book open on the table. It was Sandra. I knew right away that she was working her magic on Amir. I slowed my pace so that she would be finished talking to him by the time I arrived in front of the restaurant.

She went back inside. Amir went back to reading his book. He didn't notice me as I went through the patio area and into the restaurant.

"What's up with you?" Sandra watched me struggle as I couldn't get the milk to foam properly for the cappuccinos; my frustration was clear. I was ashamed at having created a whole story in my mind with Amir on the flimsiest of foundations. I didn't explain myself to Sandra, but I didn't need to. She knew me well enough that all she had to do was watch me carefully for the next hour to guess what was going on.

When Amir came in to use the bathroom I made a special effort to focus on polishing the cutlery while my cheeks burned. Sandra stood talking to him outside the bathroom. By the way they looked in my direction while trying to make it look like they weren't looking in my direction, I knew they were talking about me. I wanted to stab my eye out with one of the forks I was polishing, but I restrained myself.

It was a busy shift and I didn't have a chance to talk to Sandra until we were on the way home. "What were you and Amir talking about outside the bathrooms earlier?"

"Amir's okay, you know. He's not fake like Michal. He's smart and nice and doesn't try to put his hands all over you like those other assholes."

Was she trying to convince me?

I put Amir out of my mind. I knew that if Sandra wanted him there was no use trying to compete. He didn't come into the restaurant anyway until the following weekend. It was almost a carbon copy. He was on the patio talking to Sandra, I was walking along Scollard. But this time there was someone else sitting at the table with Amir. Sandra spotted me coming along the street and she called out and gestured for me to come over. Amir had brought a friend. I could tell by the way Sandra made a big show of introducing me that they had planned the whole thing. The friend was for me.

Nikola was short with thick fingers and a fake leather jacket he wore in spite of the temperature being in the mid-30s. "We're going to grab a drink before the dinner shift," Sandra told me in the locker room. "Isn't Nikola nice? You guys will get along great."

Sandra helped me fix my hair and offered to lend me her necklace. "It'll look so good with your white shirt, you've got a little bit of a tan now."

I held the necklace up to my throat. Sandra was right. It did look nice against my slightly tanned skin. I could see the picture that Sandra was painting coming into focus. She would get Amir, the good looking, interesting guy, and she would be a good friend by finding a less attractive, less interesting guy for me, her less attractive, less interesting friend.

I could see that her picture was more realistic than the one I had started to imagine of Amir and me. I didn't know whether to feel angry at her for taking Amir, or to feel grateful to her for taking the trouble to try and set me up with Nikola. Of course I had no claim to Amir. He had admired my cappuccino-making skills, but that didn't mean anything. Maybe Nikola was the best I could hope for. I tried to picture him. All I could see were his thick fingers.

After the lunch service Amir and Nikola waited for us outside the restaurant and we walked together – Sandra and Amir in front, me and Nikola behind – to Cumberland Park. I was tired from working the lunch shift and I didn't have much to say to Nikola. He talked about cars. His voice was nice, and if I didn't look at him, it was okay to walk and listen to him. We sat near the big rock.

The sun was hot, but there were some trees that provided enough shade to make it comfortable to sit. Cumberland Park was alive with the chatter of people, the cooing of pigeons, and the hum of cars trolling for an elusive parking spot. A teenager rode by on a skateboard. A woman spoke loudly into her cell phone. Through all this noise, I thought I heard someone calling my name. I discounted the possibility and assumed I had been mistaken.

"Frida? I think that guy is talking to you." Sandra had heard it too. She gestured with her chin behind me. I turned to look.

It was Lionel.

It was so strange to see Lionel outside of the allotment garden. I had only ever seen him in gardening clothes, usually covered in dirt and sweat. Now he was clean and neatly dressed in dark pants and a red polo shirt. I felt confused and embarrassed to have him see me there with Sandra, Amir and Nikola. After awkward introductions I stood up and took a couple of steps away from where we had been sitting. Lionel turned towards me so that we were a twosome, separate from the threesome of Sandra, Amir and Nikola.

"You coming from work?" I asked, realizing that maybe he was in uniform.

"Yeah. I just finished." Lionel stood still, so still he was like a rock in a quick-moving stream. I felt the nervous tension that been sitting in my chest since arriving at work earlier that day subside into a warm, pleasant feeling that flowed through my arms and legs, up the back of my head and out the tips of my hair.

"Those your friends?" he made the slightest movement with his head to indicate Sandra, Amir and Nikola.

"Sandra is my best friend. We just know those guys from the restaurant." Unlike Lionel, I couldn't stand still. I swayed from one foot to the other and reached up to fiddle with Sandra's necklace. I wanted to touch Lionel's arm or rest my head on his shoulder, but I felt I would pass out if I did that.

"It was nice to see you. I gotta get going home. My mom needs me to help her out with some stuff."

I had a momentary crazy idea that I could go with him. Help his mom. Maybe eat dinner together. We could go down to the allotment garden together before it got dark to check on the beds, pull a few weeds, give some water. But Lionel was gone. He had said goodbye to Sandra, Amir and Nikola so politely that they were left speechless. I went to sit down. Nikola took a package of cigarettes from the pocket of the ever-present leather jacket and offered me one.

"No, thanks. I'm trying to quit."

QUESTIONING

Sandra and Amir became an item. She was right, he wasn't like Michal. In fact, he never kissed her or even held her hand in public.

"He says in his country men and women don't do stuff like that in public." Sandra was really into him, I could tell. He didn't have money like Michal, but she didn't care. "He's really smart. When he's saved up some money, he's going back to school. He's going to be an engineer."

Sandra and I were laying on towels on the grass in my backyard. Maggie had made us some iced tea. It felt great to lie there in the sun with cold drinks and talk about boys.

"Where does he work, anyway?" I shielded my eyes from the sun with a floppy straw hat Maggie had lent me.

Sandra paused, "Uh, I guess they all work for Michal."

I realized that she didn't know for sure. And then I realized that I wasn't sure even what Michal did. I sat up. "Sandra, what kind of business is Michal in?"

Sandra turned over onto her stomach and took a slurp of iced tea. "Oh I don't know. Computers or something boring."

I had seen Michal with a laptop a couple of times, but mostly he just had his phone. He didn't strike me as a computer guy. Harold and Maggie's eldest son Paul worked for a software company and all I knew about his work was that he was always at the office. I had heard Harold and Maggie talking about how he would never get a girlfriend if he spent all his time in an office with a bunch of other computer guys. Paul was serious and quiet. I couldn't picture him drinking whiskey and making out with a waitress at a restaurant.

"What does Amir do for him?" I tried to sound laid back. I didn't want it to seem like I was giving Sandra the third degree.

"Amir doesn't talk about that kind of stuff with me." Sandra stretched out lazily, pointing her toes and rolling a little side to side on her stomach. She lifted her head and shoulders and rested her chin in her hands. "In fact, Amir doesn't do too much talking with me at all." The way she emphasized "talking" she wanted me to ask,

"Oh really? What do you guys do then?"

"He always wants to get in my pants. It's funny because he won't even kiss me when anyone else is around, but as soon as we are alone, he's all over me." Sandra seemed proud of this and I was jealous of her ability to have this effect on a guy. "Nikola keeps asking about you, Frida. Why don't we go out again?"

The idea of Nikola wanting to "be all over me" like Amir was with Sandra had no appeal for me. I wanted to change the subject. "What did you think of Lionel?"

"That black guy we saw in Cumberland Park? You like him?" Sandra's reaction was hard to read. She was surprised, but why? Because Lionel was black?

"I don't know, maybe just as a friend." I tried to picture Lionel and I kissing or him putting his hands on me, but I could only envision him digging in the garden or leaning against a tree to rest for a minute. But I liked to think of him. It made me feel calm and strong at the same time. I didn't know how to explain this to Sandra so I changed the subject. She got a text from Amir and said that she had to go, they were getting together in an hour.

I stayed in the backyard for a while after Sandra left. I tried to puzzle out in my mind: Michal and Amir. Nikola. Lionel. I looked up at the leaves of our maple tree. The shifting light patterns were nice to watch but they didn't provide me with any answers. I knew who I could ask about Michal and Amir at least. Tomasz.

"Computers?" Tomasz wiped the glasses before things got busy the next day. The expression on his face when I had said that Michal and Amir worked with computers was close to the one he got when customers tried to order Frappuccinos. "Maybe stolen computers," he scoffed. "Listen, Frida. You are nice girl. Sandra is also nice girl. Carly is not so nice, but you should all stay away from those guys. Just make the coffee; clear the tables. Get nice Canadian boyfriend who plays hockey. Those guys are crooks."

Sandra was dismissive. "Tomasz doesn't know shit." I didn't know what to believe.

Labour Day weekend there was a BBQ planned at the allotment garden, an end of summer celebration. I hadn't gone there too much in August because of all the hours I had been putting in at Bouillabaisse. But things at Bouillabaisse were so weird now. Carly and Michal would sit drinking and making out in the back booth. Carly had all but given up the pretence of working. Sandra kept on asking me to go out with her, Amir and Nikola and I didn't know how to say no to her.

I really wanted to go to the allotment garden to escape Bouillabaisse for a while and to see Lionel. I took the night off. Philippe was pissed because he knew it would be busy.

It was a hot day. The aging hippies and the new immigrants and the back-to-the-earth types all mingled together comparing harvests and chasing wasps away from the food. I knew Lionel wouldn't be coming until later, he had work. His mom Teresa had brought potato salad and was dishing it out. "I bet you're glad to be going back to school next week." Teresa was generous with her servings of potato salad and with her opinions of people. She would always find the best quality of someone and highlight it. If the good quality was hard to see, she would exaggerate it in a way that made the person believe they could live up to her opinion. She had decided that I was good in school, and always encouraged me when we spoke. School was not top of my mind, but when Teresa assumed that I was looking forward to going back, I felt that maybe I was.

"Lionel is sure happy to be going back. He worked thirty hours a week at that sport store, even though they didn't treat him right." Teresa went on to explain which courses Lionel was taking the following year, what his options were for jobs once he finished his community activity program. She told me that they planned to rent a car in the spring and drive up to a tree farm near Uxbridge to get some good shrubs for the allotment garden. The picture she painted of Lionel was warm and clear. There were no dark corners or surreal elements. I smiled as I listened to her.

It was almost six by the time Lionel arrived. I was tired from having spent the day in the sun. I was resting on an old garden lounger someone had brought. It was a bit rickety, but I was light enough that I felt confident it would not fall apart under me.

"I see you're letting other people work for a change." I hadn't heard him approaching, I might have been half asleep.

"We finished all the potato salad."

"That's alright. We got more at home." Lionel put out his hand to help me up from my reclining position. His hand was strong and steady. We walked around the allotment gardens for a while. People were tidying up, saying goodbye. Lionel and I avoided goodbye by continuing to walk. Teresa left. The sun started to go down.

"Do you want to walk up to Queen Street and get something to eat?"

I told Lionel everything. About Carly, about Sandra and Amir. I told him about Nikola even though my cheeks burned as I did. Lionel listened and nodded. The only comment he made was when I told him what Tomasz said about Michal and Amir being crooks.

"It's easy to judge people. Maybe they are crooks, but that might not be the whole story. You have to know yourself whether they are people you want to be around or not." I wished I knew. I had so many different ideas in my head, I couldn't keep them straight. I wished Teresa could paint me into a nice clear picture like the one she had done of Lionel.

The day in the sun, the emotion of my talk with Lionel, it was all too much. I sat down on the curb just before Queen Street, put my head in my hands and started to cry. Lionel sat beside me and put his hand on my shoulder. We were sitting like this for a few minutes when a police car came to a stop in front of us.

A middle-aged cop got out of the car. "What seems to be the problem?" Lionel slowly removed his hand from my shoulder. He rested both his arms on his knees and stretched his hands out in front of him, palms up.

"No problem, officer. She's just a little tired." The cop looked at Lionel. He shifted his weight back and forth from one foot to another. I noticed all the gear he had strapped to him, "He must be hot," I thought.

"Are you okay, young lady? Is this guy bothering you?" The question confused me. I sensed Lionel going tense beside me.

When I didn't answer, he persisted, "Do you know this young man?" I nodded.

"Alright, stand up please. I'd like to see some ID." The cop took a step back and rested his hand on his gun. Lionel sighed and then got up slowly.

"My ID is in my back pocket. Can I reach for it?" I looked up at Lionel. He was talking like you would to a scared kid. He held his hands out from his body with his palms up, facing the cop.

"Why don't you step over here beside the car first. Miss, I'd like you to go and sit down on the other side of the street, please. I'll come and talk to you in a minute." I moved where he had told me like a zombie. From where I sat on the other side of the street I could see the cop standing with his hand on his gun. They were talking for a couple of minutes. I saw the cop gesture towards me. I saw Lionel gesture towards the allotment gardens. Lionel reached for his ID in his back pocket. The cop took it from him and took out his notebook and wrote in it while leaning against the car. Lionel stood watching him. He didn't look at me.

Finally the cop came across the street to talk to me. "Do you know this young man?" he asked me again. I felt like this was a trick question. I did know Lionel, but did I really know him? Had he done something wrong? What was the right answer?

"Yes. I know him. His name is Lionel. I met him at the allotment gardens." The cop had no reaction to this. "Do your parents know that you're out with Lionel?" I thought about Harold and Maggie. They knew all about the allotment garden and Lionel and Teresa, but they technically didn't know that I was with him at that exact moment.

"Well, no, but they would be fine with it if they knew." I started to feel angry. What was this guy's problem?

"If you're sure you are okay I will let you get on your way. But if you need any help here, don't be afraid to ask."

I was sure that this cop was not going to be able to give me the help that I needed. "I'd like to go back to my friend now."

"Take care, miss. Have a nice evening." He got back in his car and drove off. I looked across the street at Lionel. He tilted his head to one side in a question. I lifted my hands and shrugged "beats me". He beckoned for me to come across.

"What the hell was that?" I reached out to hold Lionel's hand or arm. He didn't reach back.

"I guess you don't get questioned by police too often." Lionel's voice had a hardness to it that I had never heard before. In the deep background of my mind were the flashing police lights and the cold air biting my skin through my pyjamas.

I looked at my feet and mumbled, "no."

Lionel was quiet for a minute. We had started walking again and had reached Queen Street by this time. Lionel stopped and turned to look at me. It was dusk. He looked so beautiful with the evening light on his kind face. "Frida, I've been questioned eight times by police just this summer. I almost lost my job because they held me for questioning for two hours one day." What could I say? I just told him how sorry I was.

"I'm just gonna head home now," Lionel gestured towards the streetcar stop.

"I'll text you later?" I didn't want to let him go.

"You don't have to." Lionel walked away.

I went to a coffee shop to give him a chance to get on the streetcar. I ordered an iced tea. I guess I looked a wreck because the girl behind the counter gave me the drink for free.

BAD VIBES

———— ı|ıı ————

W hen I got home I went straight to bed. Maggie had to wake me at ten the next day. I couldn't understand for a minute why the alarm on my phone hadn't gone off and then I remembered that my phone battery had died at midday and I hadn't put it to charge when I got home. I was scheduled to work brunch at Bouillabaisse. I needed to get going.

I turned on the shower and plugged in the phone. The water ran down my back and neck as I went over in my mind the events of the day before. I felt like I was to blame for the cop stopping to question Lionel. If I hadn't been crying like a fool. Over what? My worries over Carly and Michal, Sandra, Amir and Nikola all seemed so stupid compared with Lionel getting questioned by cops eight times. Eight times! For what? Lionel was the definition of goodness. He was absolutely the last guy police should be questioning.

When I got out of the shower I had several messages that Sandra had sent the night before. I stood wrapped in a towel as I read them:

5 p.m. have fun at BBQ! miss you!

6:23 p.m. busy night lots of tourists Carly a no show : (

7:45 p.m. bad vibes with Michal and Amir. assholes. msg me

What was going on? I got dressed and left the house. It was the day before Labour Day. The weather was hot and humid and the thunderstorm that threatens every late August day was building clouds over the lake. I couldn't get a hold of Sandra. She wasn't responding to my texts. The air conditioning was out on the subway I caught. By the time I got to Yorkville, I was sweaty and wilted.

Sandra and Amir were standing in the alleyway where we had seen Carly and Michal kissing that first time. Sandra and Amir weren't kissing, in fact it looked like they were having an argument.

"Why don't you just admit you were with Carly? Obviously the two of you are in on everything." Sandra was shouting. Amir was quiet and reacted to Sandra's outburst by shaking his head and walking away, down the alleyway towards where I was standing. There was no way for me to pretend that I hadn't heard, so I just stood there awkwardly. Amir didn't seem bothered.

"Hello, Frida. Hot day today." He walked past me and turned onto Yorkville Avenue.

I went to Sandra. "What happened? Are you okay?"

"What an asshole! Does he think I'm an idiot?" Sandra vibrated with anger.

"You're going to have to fill me in." Was Amir sleeping with Carly now? I was totally confused. Sandra and I sat side by side on the stoop of a the back door of a stationary shop that opened onto the alleyway. Sandra told me the whole story and I listened without speaking, just nodding to show I understood.

"So Carly doesn't show up for work and everyone's running around like crazy because we are busy and down you and Carly. I had been trying to get hold of Amir all day, but he just ghosted me. Finally he turns up with Michal and the two of them are sitting in the back booth, but they're not really talking. Michal looks super mad and Amir is sitting like he got caught skipping school.

"So then Carly texts me: 'Is Michal there?'

I'm like 'Yeah. Where the f r u'

'Some serious shit going down with Michal' I don't even want to know, so I don't reply.

"Then I start thinking maybe she was with Amir and Michal found out and now she's avoiding Michal and Amir knows that Michal knows and is waiting to see what he'll do, and maybe she's texting me to see if I know! So then I march up to the booth to confront Amir and I go 'What the hell is going on?' Amir is all scared and says 'This is not a good time Sandra. I will talk to you later.' I'm not going to take that, so I go 'No, you'll talk to me now. Why didn't you return my texts all day?' And then fucking Michal pipes up, 'Little girl. This is none of your business. Go away and wash dishes or whatever it is you do here. The men are talking.'

"I didn't even know what to say. I just left those two assholes and I told Tomasz I was going outside for a smoke break. So now I'm standing in the alleyway fuming about Michal and Amir and some dude comes up and goes 'hey, you work at the restaurant?' I say that I do and I can see that he's not a customer, I'm thinking he's looking for a food handout or work or something, but no! 'Is Carly working tonight?' he goes. What is with this bitch? How many guys is she doing? 'No,' I tell him, 'she's not here tonight.' 'Okay,' he goes, 'tell her Brian came by.' I tell him sure and off he goes. When I go back in the restaurant Michal and Amir are gone, Philippe is freaking out because basically he has no staff and I'm just pissed because I don't know what is going on!"

I had never seen Sandra like this. She was like a different person, and although she may have been mad because she suspected Amir was messing around with Carly, what really pissed her off what not knowing what was going on. Being treated like she didn't matter. Being called "little girl" by Michal. I could tell that was what really got to her. I tried to calm her down.

"I don't know what's going on either Sandra. Maybe it's something totally unrelated to you and Amir. Brunch is starting soon. Let's just go and work and then we'll go grab ice cream before the evening shift."

Sandra stood up and checked her phone. If she had heard me she didn't acknowledge what I said. "Carly better show up tonight. She's got some explaining to do."

We went into work.

BRIAN

———— ı|ı| ————

N one of the Albanians came for brunch. It wasn't too busy so Sandra and I could take breaks to enjoy the afternoon sun. I tried to text Lionel, but he didn't reply. Now that I was back at Bouillabaisse with Sandra, the emotions of the day before were less vivid. Her anger cancelled out whatever I might have been feeling.

Tomasz tried talking to her. "Forget about Amir. Maybe he is charming and good looking, but you need nice Canadian boyfriend." Sandra and I laughed at this idea Tomasz had about Canadian boys who play hockey being the only legitimate boyfriend material for us. The only hockey-playing guys we knew were barely able to put a sentence together and they would never talk to us. We might have been from the same school, but we were worlds apart.

When I looked through the yearbook I felt like I was looking at some alternate reality. There was exactly one picture of me and Sandra. We happened to be walking by when a picture of the cross-country running team was being taken.

The yearbook photographer had spotted Sandra and asked if we wanted to have our picture taken. Sandra looked mysterious and glamorous; she was wearing sunglasses and a tight-fitting top. I looked hopelessly awkward. I was squinting because I didn't have my sunglasses with me and I was wearing a goofy t-shirt with a picture of a dog on it that Harold had got for me. The caption on the picture was something like "friends 'til the end", and I actually thought that was a very generous caption because they could have put something like "odd couple" or "beauty and the beast."

Brunch wrapped up easily and we went to grab ice cream and wander around Yorkville before the evening shift. Sandra's mood had improved. We had made good tips and we knew that Bouillabaisse was closed for Labour Day so we would have a day to relax before school started.

"I think I'm going to tell Philippe that I'm not going to keep working once school starts." Sandra had ordered black cherry ice cream and was assiduously picking out the cherries to eat first. "We can get a job at a clothing store then we can get a discount on nice clothes." I didn't know how to feel about this, obviously having nice clothes would be a good idea, but Bouillabaisse had become like a second home for me. Philippe was still angry and would sometimes tell us off, but we knew that he treated everyone the same and worked harder than anyone else. Francois couldn't remember our names and just called us "les filles", but with affection. He would encourage us to take home leftover food. "Make a good change from Kraft Dinner, no?" which maybe was meant to be an insult, but we didn't get it. Tomasz had become like a brother to me. He was so proud that he had been the one to teach me how to use the espresso machine because now I was the undisputed cappuccino queen. Some customers would go elsewhere for their coffee if I wasn't working.

Sandra and I planned what we would buy with the money we had made at Bouillabaisse over the summer. We were feeling pretty good. We joked about blowing all our savings on one Chanel bag. "I'll just wear a garbage bag, but if I'm carrying the bag, everyone will be impressed." Sandra mimed walking into school being worn by a designer handbag. We laughed and laughed in the sun until it was time for the dinner shift.

Just before arriving back at the restaurant, Sandra grabbed my arm and turned her head and shielded her mouth with her hand in order to talk to me. "Be casual. Look over there, by the white SUV." When I did as she said, I saw a tall guy who looked like he was just a couple of years older than us. He was standing on the sidewalk talking on his phone. He was wearing a camouflage jacket and had close cropped reddish hair and a mean face. He was very intent on his phone call, so he didn't notice us. "That's the dude who was looking for Carly last night. That's Brian."

When we got to the restaurant, Sandra and I went to the locker room. Carly was there. Sandra wasted no time, "where the hell were you last night? It was chaos here!"

Carly looked up from her phone; she clearly had no idea what Sandra was talking about. "Did you talk to Amir today?" It was like she hadn't heard Sandra.

"It's none of your business whether I did or I didn't. What's the matter? Can't keep all of your boyfriends straight? Your other one is out on Scollard right now." Sandra tried to play it cool, but I could see that she was mad.

"Michal?" Carly looked confused.

"No. Brian."

Carly's expression changed into something I had never seen in her. She paled so much that her freckles stood out like chicken pox on her skin. "Tell me you're joking. Brian? Where?" She had dropped her phone and was gripping Sandra's arm. Sandra was taken aback. She explained that we had seen him outside and that he had been there the night before looking for her.

"Oh shit." Carly left the locker room, went into Philippe's office and closed the door. Sandra watched her go and then looked at me and shrugged. Tables needed to be set, bread needed to be cut, glasses needed to be wiped. Understanding what the deal was with Brian would have to wait.

Carly actually worked that evening. She was super jumpy and made sure to get the rear section of the restaurant. Every time the door opened she would jerk her head up from what she was doing to see who was coming in. The majority of tables had been served by nine o'clock. The thunderstorm that had been threatening all day started to rumble and the wind picked up. Philippe asked me to tie up the umbrellas on the patio so they wouldn't get damaged in the storm.

Yorkville was pretty quiet. The rich had gone to their cottages, Tomasz said, and the tourists had gone to the Ex. Only one car passed while I was out on the patio: a white SUV with Quebec plates. It drove slowly by as I wrestled with the umbrellas and the first drops of rain fell.

I went down to the locker room to brush my hair that had been blown out of order on the patio. Carly was there looking an absolute nervous wreck. I had never liked her, but I could help feel sorry for whatever was freaking her out.

"You didn't see Brian out there did you?" Carly was sitting on her hands and I had a feeling it was to stop them from shaking.

"There was nobody out there, Carly. A storm's coming. We'll probably close early tonight." I tried to sound reassuring. Carly nodded. "Who is that Brian guy, anyway?"

Carly looked through me and said with pain, "He's my brother."

"Oh shit, Carly. Are you for real? Why are you so nervous about him?" I couldn't stop myself from asking. Harold and

Maggie's boys, who were technically my brothers might be embarrassing or annoying, but I could see that for Carly, the idea of her brother turning up at Bouillabaisse was terrifying.

"Frida, my brother is not a nice guy. Wherever he goes, trouble follows." Carly's phone buzzed and she snatched it from the chair beside her. Relief washed over her face. "It's Michal. He just got here."

I finished fixing my hair and we both went back to the dining room. Michal, Amir and two other guys had arrived and were sitting at the big table in the centre of the dining room. Their usual back booth was taken by two couples who were taking their time over steaks and red wine.

Carly sat beside Michal right away and started talking to him earnestly. I couldn't hear what she was saying, but I assumed it was about Brian. I saw Sandra working the espresso machine and I went over to her.

"Brian is Carly's brother." I filled the coffee bean grinder while dropping my bombshell.

Sandra was floored. She almost dropped the milk jug and a jet of steam shot out scalding her hand. "Shit!" She went to the sink to run it under cold water. "That is wild, Frida! Why is she acting so weird?"

"I don't know. She just said that he's not a nice guy."

I could see that Michal was now talking to Carly, and her face was full of fear again. Whatever he was telling her, it was not calming her down. I wanted to know what he was saying. I walked past the table with open ears.

"What do you mean? Are you nuts? You don't know him!" Carly wasn't trying to keep her voice down. She got up from the table and went towards the locker room. Michal, Amir and the other two spoke quietly together.

Carly stayed downstairs for maybe ten minutes. I wanted to hear more, so I took my time clearing a table that had just left near the front of the restaurant. I had cleared it pretty well and was awkwardly trying to find an excuse to stay near Michal's table. I looked over to the bar to see if I could catch Sandra's eye, but she wasn't there anymore. I noticed that there were some bread crumbs on the floor. Normally I wouldn't bother, but this time I crouched down and, using a napkin, started to sweep the crumbs up.

From that vantage point I could only see the people around me from the waist down. I recognized Carly's legs as she came upstairs with her bag. She was going to leave! I watched her walk towards Michal's table. Just as she approached the table, the front door of the restaurant opened. A gust of wind blew in and I looked to see who it was. The legs I saw wore black jeans and black boots with no laces. The legs took three steps inside the restaurant and then I heard a loud popping sound. I looked back towards Carly and I saw her crumple to the floor. The door opened again, the black jean legs left. People started screaming. Carly lay on the restaurant floor and a spot of blood was widening on the right side of her chest. I started to crawl towards her, but a bunch of other legs came between me and her, so I just sat stunned until Sandra came and picked me up off the floor.

DETECTIVE

T he police called Harold to come and get me.

After the gun shots there was so much noise and confusion. Philippe had been the first one to reach Carly and he had tried to stop the bleeding with a linen napkin, but it quickly became soaked with blood and Carly didn't respond to him calling her name in a desperate voice.

Several customers called 911. In the few minutes between the noise and confusion immediately following the gun shots and the arrival of the police and ambulance, there was an eerie quiet. Philippe stopped calling Carly's name and just held her head in his lap and murmured to himself in French. The noise that would usually come from the kitchen was silent as all the cook staff stood by the bar with shocked faces, their whites stained with sauce. One elderly lady who had been dining alone had started to panic, but Tomasz had managed to calm her down by bringing her a tea and reassuring her that everything was alright, the police would be here soon. Now he stood by her without speaking.

My heart was racing. I sat on the floor holding on to Sandra and I could feel the blood pumping in my ears. I tried to make sense of the scene that was in front of my eyes, but I was having a hard time. Why was Carly on the floor covered in blood? She's been shot: I reasoned to myself. This seemed to be the only fact that I could hang onto. One other thing registered less clearly, but it was there: Michal, Amir and the other two guys that had been at the table with them were nowhere to be seen.

When the police and the ambulance did arrive they moved us all away from the dining room. Sandra, Tomasz, Philippe and I were all put in Philippe's office with a cop in uniform. He was younger then I thought cops usually were. I remembered the middle-aged guy who had questioned me and Lionel. This younger guy seemed a little bored to be sitting with us waiting for something to happen. He took an elastic band from Philippe's desk and stretched it between his fingers over and over again. He told us all to sit down and relax, that someone would come and take our statements soon. He was the one who called Harold.

"No, sir, your daughter hasn't been injured. She's had a bad shock, but she's okay. We're going to want to take a statement from her. Can you please come down to the restaurant?"

When Harold arrived, I was glad to see him and gave him a hug even though we didn't hug normally. His thinning hair was standing up straight all over his head and there was a tightness around his jaw and an edge to his voice when he asked the young cop, "Can I take her home now?"

"They're going to want to take her statement. Shouldn't be too long now."

Harold let out a sigh and joined us in the cramped office. He saw Sandra. "Is your mom coming down?"

"Oh yeah. She's on her way." I looked at Sandra for confirmation because I knew that the young cop had not been able to get a hold of Sandra's mother and neither had Sandra. She returned my questioning look with blank eyes. "Listen, when can we get out of here. I can't sit here much longer." I could see that Sandra was winding herself up for a fight.

"Shouldn't be too much longer." The young cop didn't react to Sandra's impatience. He just kept stretching that elastic.

Philippe and Tomasz started talking about who would clean up the kitchen. Harold seemed ready to nod off. Finally a woman cop came to the door.

At first I thought she was a social worker. She wasn't wearing a uniform and she had that rumpled, caring look about her that social workers have. But no, "I'm detective Aquino. I'm going to be leading the investigation." When she spoke I could tell she wasn't a social worker. She didn't have that sort of gentle questioning in her voice that social workers always have. Her authority took up a lot of space in that already crowded office. "Officer Wright, please take these people out of here while I talk to the young lady who was under the table when the shooter came in." That was me, I realized. I felt immediately that it was suspicious that I should have been under the table. I felt Harold look at me questioningly. Philippe, Sandra and Tomasz left with the young cop and detective Aquino, Harold and I stayed in Philippe's office. The detective sat behind the desk and opened her notebook.

"Frida, I know you have had a terrible shock here tonight, so we'll try to keep this brief. Just tell me in your own words what happened."

I tried to explain how I had been clearing the table, I didn't mention that I had been intentionally taking my time in order to eavesdrop on Michal and Carly's argument, and that I had been crouching down to sweep up the bread crumbs when I felt the door open.

"Now try and describe exactly what you saw."

I closed my eyes. I could see the floor with the bread crumbs, my hand with the napkin and the legs of the table. "I felt the wind when the door opened so I looked over to see who was coming in."

"Did you stand up?"

"No. I stayed crouched down."

"Fine. Continue."

"All I saw was a pair of legs."

"Just one pair of legs?"

I thought for a minute. Yes, there had only been one pair of legs.

"Can you describe the legs for me?"

Harold patted my arm, "You're doing great."

"They were a man's legs, I'm pretty sure. Wearing black jeans and black boots."

"Black boots? Like Doc Martens?"

"No. No laces. Like Blunstones." Detective Aquino made a note.

"Then what?"

"I heard the shots and I saw Carly fall to the floor." In my mind's eye I saw it again: the sudden crumpling, the red stain on her chest.

"Did you notice anything else?"

"No. Things went crazy after that with everyone screaming and trying to help Carly."

"How well did you know Carly?"

"Not too well. We've been working here together for a few months, but we weren't really friends."

"Was there anything strange about the way Carly was behaving tonight?"

"I knew she was really upset about her brother coming to see her."

"Have you met her brother?"

"No."

"Why was Carly upset about her brother coming?"

"She said he was bad news."

"Did she say why?"

"No. Like I said, we weren't really friends, but I could tell she was really freaked out about her brother coming."

"And did he come?"

"I'm not sure."

"Frida. Do you think it was Carly's brother who shot her?" Detective Aquino posed this terrible question with absolute calm. She looked at me as if I had the answer. As if I could know who had done this thing.

"I don't know." It was the only possible answer.

Detective Aquino asked a few more questions, but I guess I looked ready to pass out, so she told Harold to take me home and that she would contact us again to get a formal statement. I felt wobbly, like the time at grade six sports day from too much heat and not enough water. Harold thanked the detective. "Let's get you home", he put his arm around my shoulders. I got my stuff from the locker room where Sandra, Tomasz and Philippe were sitting awkwardly with the young cop. We went out to the car and drove silently home to North York.

When we got home Harold told me to go to bed, that we would talk things over in the morning. He looked tired, older. I thanked him and went up to my room. I couldn't sleep. The images of those legs and boots and Carly crumpling to the floor kept on appearing whenever I closed my eyes. I could hear that Harold hadn't gone straight to bed. I heard the sound of a cupboard door opening and closing and then ice in a glass. This was strange. Was Harold having an iced tea in the middle of the night? The temperature had dropped a lot with the storm. It was unlike Harold.

I got out of bed quietly and went to see what he was doing. He didn't hear me come part of the way down the stairs in my bare feet. He was sitting at the dining room table with what was obviously a bottle of alcohol in front of him. I had never seen Harold drink, not even a beer, so this sight was enough to stop me halfway down the staircase. He drained the glass. Then he got up and put the bottle away in the back of a cupboard where Maggie kept the nice china we never used. He washed his glass carefully and put it away.

I went back to my room. I waited until I heard Harold come upstairs and get into bed. When I was sure he would be asleep, I went back downstairs. I opened the cupboard and took out the bottle. Canadian Club Rye Whiskey. I got a glass, but I didn't take a chance with clinking ice cubes. I poured myself a drink the size I had seen Michal and Amir drink at Bouillabaisse. The smell was sharp and made my eyes water. I took a tentative sip. The burning sensation was immediate, but I didn't cough or choke. I just swallowed and took a few breaths. The warmth spread from my throat almost immediately, and I took another sip. This one burned less. One sip at a time I drank the rye whiskey sitting in Harold and Maggie's dining room. The images of the legs, of Carly, of Detective Aquino's questioning eyes started to cycle more slowly in my brain. The sound of the shots, of Philippe calling Carly's name in that desperate voice, those sounds faded too as I drank.

Eventually, I put the bottle away, washed the glass carefully and went up to bed.

LABOUR DAY

The relaxing Labour Day Sandra and I had anticipated was now a day of shocked recovery. I slept fitfully for twelve hours, periodically I would hear a phone ringing or sense that Maggie had come into my room and was looking at me, but then I would be pulled back into a restless sleep. When Maggie finally told me it was time to get up, my sheets were twisted and damp with sweat. I felt raw and shaky and my mouth had a peculiar metallic taste that I figured must be due to the rye.

Maggie made me toast and tea for breakfast and we sat without talking at the dining room table. I sensed that Maggie wanted to comfort me, but she felt unsure of what to say. None of their boys had been involved in anything this serious. It felt so odd to be sitting in the quiet house with Maggie drinking tea. A part of me felt that maybe the whole thing had been a dream.

Maggie watched me drink my tea and eat my toast and this normalcy seemed to give her the confidence to speak. She adopted the matter of fact tone that she used whenever faced with problems. In her life, up until now, any problem had a clear solution that, once decided on, was to be acted on without fuss. Car broken down? "That's alright. We'll call for a tow." Illness? "You'll be alright. We'll just call Dr. Bastedo." Bad haircut? "It's fine. Just wear a hat until it grows out."

Obviously this situation was more delicate than those that Maggie normally dealt with, but this strategy worked for her and so it's what she adopted now. "We'll just go to the station and give your statement. You'll be fine." Maggie cleared the dishes and stood drying her hands on a teacloth.

"I already told them that I didn't see who it was."

"It's alright. Other people were there too. What you saw is just one piece of the puzzle. It's not up to you to find out who did it. You just say what you saw." Maggie folded the teacloth and hung it on the handle of the stove. "Detective Aquino called this morning. She said to come to the station at 3:00 p.m. Go get dressed and I'll take you there."

It was a relief to have Maggie tell me what to do. I went up to my room. I had taken off my work clothes the night before and left them in a crumpled heap on the floor. Seeing the black pants and white shirt now was a reminder of the events of the night before. The restaurant smell still clung to them as I picked them up and buried them at the bottom of my laundry hamper.

Maggie and I drove in silence to the police station. I wondered if Sandra would be there too. I hadn't heard anything from her and I didn't know what I would say if I saw her.

No one else from the restaurant was at the police station when we got there.

SOUP

———— ı|ı| ————

Sandra and I met up to go to school the next day. There were no classes, we just had to pick up our timetables. Even in high school, they still printed them on that same pink paper I remembered from the first day we met. That had been almost four years ago. We had been twelve years old. Now we were sixteen and we had witnessed a murder.

I looked at Sandra. I knew her so well I felt like I could read her every expression and gesture. Sometimes, like now, I looked at her like a stranger would. I could see that she was beautiful. She had passed through the phase when she wore a lot of makeup. Now she just did her eyes with a little black eyeliner. She had pierced her left eyebrow and wore a small silver ring there. She had developed a woman's body over the past four years. I was still thin and child like. Puberty had brought my period and body hair, but not much in the way of womanly curves. I had always been hopeless at applying makeup and the only piercings I had were in my earlobes.

Sandra would praise my slender body, "you can wear anything!" and I felt that my hair could look nice if I took the time to blow dry and straighten it so that it hung in a shiny curtain. The summer sun had brought out some blond streaks in the brown.

After picking up our timetables we went to find a place where we could sit and talk. Neither of us wanted to go home and neither of us proposed going down to Yorkville. We realized that we didn't have a place to hang out in North York. We wanted to avoid kids from school so that ruled out a few spots.

"Let's go to Lieberman's." Sandra's mom had taken us to Lieberman's a few times. It was a Jewish family diner in a strip mall on Bathurst. We were not likely to run into anyone from school there.

"Perfect."

Lieberman's had wonderful soup, fresh bagels and an ancient waitress with teased, dyed-blonde hair who called us "my dears" and sat us at the counter since the tables were all full, mainly with old men nursing cups of coffee.

"I can't believe that Carly's dead." Sandra stirred her soup to cool it off. "What did the cops ask you?"

"They just wanted to know what I saw and what I knew about Carly."

"What did you tell them?"

"Just the truth. That I saw the feet come in the restaurant and then I saw Carly go down."

"Did you tell them about Brian being her brother?"

"Yeah, and that Carly had been freaked out about seeing him."

Sandra took a slurp of soup. I decided that since she was asking me a bunch of questions, I could ask one too. "Where were you when she got shot?"

Sandra took another slurp and then put her spoon down and leaned her head towards me. "I was taking dishes to the dishpit to be be washed. I heard the shots and people screaming so I came running, but the shooter had already left. I didn't see him," Sandra brought her head even closer to mine and lowered her voice to a whisper, "but I know who shot her." This was not a surprise to me, Sandra always knew.

I knew the answer, but I wanted Sandra to be the one to say that it had been Brian. She didn't stop there, "And I know why, too."

This was unexpected. I knew that Carly and Sandra hung out sometimes, but that was before Michal came on the scene, and I had been the one to tell Sandra that Brian was Carly's brother. I had never doubted Sandra, but now I had to look at her to see if she was being real. She had returned to her soup. She had a half smile that I recognized from when she gave teachers made up excuses for missed school assignments. Sandra didn't know who had killed Carly, and she couldn't stand not knowing.

Just then a message came through on Sandra's phone. She jumped to check it and looked a little disappointed to tell me "it's my mom, she says the shooting is on the news." Sandra's mom had sent a link to a CP24 story. There was a uniform cop standing in front of Bouillabaisse, and there was yellow police tape across the entrance. The reporter spoke into a hand held microphone. Cars and people could be seen passing along the street behind the reporter. People living their lives as though it was a normal day.

"Last night a high end Yorkville restaurant was the scene of a deadly shooting. A young woman has been killed and police are searching for at least one suspect. I'm here with Sergeant Archero, spokesperson for the Toronto Police. Sergeant Archero, what can you tell us about what happened here last night?"

This cop was someone I had never seen before. He had a slightly crooked nose, like a hockey player, and visible acne scars, but his voice was absolutely calm and gave the details with a detached authority that was reassuring in its lack of emotion.

"Saturday night at approximately 10:40 p.m., one individual entered the Bouillabaisse restaurant on Scollard Street in the Yorkville neighbourhood. Disregarding the safety of diners and restaurant staff, this individual discharged a weapon three times and then left the premises on foot. Tragically, one person was struck by a bullet and was pronounced dead at the scene. We are not releasing the name of this individual at this time, but I can tell you that the victim was an eighteen-year-old employee of the restaurant. We are searching for a white male suspect approximately twenty to twenty-five years of age. At the time of the shooting, the suspect was wearing all black clothing, black jeans, black boots, a lightweight bomber-type jacket and a black baseball cap. We believe that the victim may not have been the intended target of the shooting and we would like to speak to anyone who was at or around Bouillabaisse restaurant on Saturday evening...."

Sandra xed out of the video and put her phone in her pocket. We sat in silence for a minute. To hear the brutal facts reported like that made it feel more unreal, like something that had happened somewhere else.

Sandra was agitated. She didn't eat any more soup. She was feverishly texting and I could see the colour rising on her cheeks. She got up and told me that she had to go. I didn't know what to say. I wanted her to stay, but I could see she was already gone. I watched her walk out the door of the diner. Her phone rang just as she was leaving and I could see her talking on the phone as she walked away.

The blonde waitress came over. "Are you finished, my dear?" I told her yes and asked for the check. "Here you go, honey." She took her order pad from her apron pocket and tore off the slip with our order. She sensed that there was something wrong. She laid the slip on the counter almost tenderly. "Don't worry, my dear. Friends always fight. You are young, you can make new friends. Or maybe you two will make up?" I looked at her. Her eyes were kind, but she had finished dispensing wisdom and was ready to wipe the counter.

I decided to walk home from Lieberman's. It was still warm and the walk was calming. In my head I went over the events of the night Carly was shot again and again. Certain things were clear in my mind. The crumbs on the floor. The black boots. The gust of air when the door opened. The blood on Carly's chest. Other things became less clear as I tried to remember them. Had Carly been sitting with Michal and Amir when the shooter came in? What had I heard her say to Michal? Had I seen Brian outside the restaurant when I went to tie up the umbrellas? Where had Michal and Amir gone after the shooting?

I wanted to stop thinking about it, but I couldn't. A part of me wanted to go down to Yorkville, but I had promised Harold and Maggie that I would be home by four and stay home that evening.

It occurred to me that there was someone who might be able to help me sort out what had happened. I had to talk to Tomasz.

TOMASZ'S ADVICE
AND MATH CLASS

I waited until I got home before calling Tomasz. It was still early so Harold and Maggie weren't home yet. The house was quiet. I sat in the dining room for a while looking out the window at the back yard. Harold and Maggie were not big gardeners. The yard was just grass, low maintenance shrubs and geraniums in pots. I felt an urge to go and prepare a bed like they had at the allotment gardens. Thinking about the allotment gardens made me think about Lionel, which made my chest ache. I wondered if he had seen the shooting in the news and connected the name of the restaurant to me. I looked at my phone and wished for him to text me. My phone stayed stubbornly silent. I went up to my room and stretched out on my bed with my F-shaped pillow. I called Tomasz.

"Frida?"

"Hi Tomasz." It was difficult to know how to talk to Tomasz because our usual workplace banter that was so effortless didn't fit with the weight of this conversation. Thankfully, Tomasz took the lead.

"You must be feeling very bad about what is happening to Carly." Tomasz sounded tired. I could hear some music playing in the background. I wondered if he was at home.

"I keep going over things in my head and then I heard the news report and it seemed so unreal. I just don't know what to think." Tomasz didn't say anything. I hugged my F pillow and tried to keep my voice steady. "Sandra is being so weird. She won't talk to me. She says she knows who killed Carly and why, but I don't even know what I saw that night!" Again, Tomasz didn't say anything, and I heard him take a drag of his cigarette. I waited. "Tomasz? What do you think happened?"

Tomasz sighed. "Listen, Frida. You remember what I told you about those guys, Michal and Amir, and how you should stay away? This is why I am telling you. They are not good people. I don't know what happened. I know that it has nothing to do with me, and nothing to do with you, and probably nothing to do with Carly."

"You think whoever came that night was trying to shoot at Michal and Amir?"

"I don't know. I am not police. But it is possible."

I let this sink in. "I'm going to go now, Tomasz. Thanks for talking."

"Okay, Frida. Take care of yourself. Tell Sandra to stay away from those guys. She should be careful."

Classes started the next day. Sandra and I were both in period one math. It was a relief to think about the usual first day of school practicalities: getting my locker, figuring out where my classes were, digging out my notebooks, pens, pencils and other tools of learning. I looked at the other students and felt completely disconnected from them. Some of them must have heard about the shooting because I was being looked at and voices were lowered as I walked by.

I was slow getting to period one, so when I got there the only seats available were in the first two rows. Sandra wasn't there yet. I sat down as quickly as I could, got out my stuff and did my best imitation of a student keen to learn the mysteries of quadratic equations. Maggie must have notified the school about what had happened because when the teacher came in he made a point of coming up to me.

Mr. Vakarovsky was an old-school teacher with a thick Russian accent. He was always rumpled: rumpled hair, rumpled clothes, rumpled papers. Somehow crystal clear math calculations emanated from that rumpled head and the students revered him. He would drill us hard so that we were almost in tears, but the concept would finally click and we would earn what was the closest thing to praise Vakarovsky would give: "Good. Now you see."

Vakarovsky probably hadn't paid too much attention in the "how to help students dealing with traumatic events" session because his strategy to offer me comfort was to come up to me in front of the whole class and announce loudly, "Frida, (he pronounced my name Fry-da and had done since grade nine) I am sorry to hear about terrible event in restaurant." I muttered thanks. "Now you will focus on math. You will feel better. You will see."

I doubted that I would be able to focus on math, but Mr. Vakarovsky's absolute conviction that math would make me feel better was comforting.

Sandra arrived late and sat at the desk next to me. Mr. Vakarovsky by this time was absorbed in his lesson and did not stop to offer Sandra sympathy. Sandra did not take out a notebook or a pencil. She sat with her phone in her lap and stared blankly at Mr. Vakarovsky as he wrote out equations on the white board. I offered her a piece of paper and a pencil, but she didn't write anything.

Sandra had only been there about twenty minutes when a message came through on her phone. I looked at her questioningly. She gave back my paper and pencil, told Mr. Vakarovsky that she wasn't feeling well and left the classroom. She gave me a look and quick gesture to let me know that she would text me later and she was gone.

When class was done I checked my phone. There was one message from Sandra:

Going to see Amir. Talk later.

FUNERAL

I was anxious about Sandra all day. She never came back to school and she didn't send me any more messages. Some other teachers and even some students tried to talk to me and offer sympathy. I just said thanks and kept my head down. I never paid as close attention to actual lessons as I did that day. Usually I would be chatting with Sandra or thinking about work, but both of those things were impossible now. I decided that Vakarovsky's suggestion to "focus on math" had been a good one.

A text finally did come through at the end of the school day. It wasn't from Sandra. It was from Philippe to all the staff. Carly's funeral will be Saturday at 2 p.m. All Bouillabaise staff are invited.

The only funeral I had been to was for Harold's dad who had been in a senior's home with Alzheimer's for most of the time I had lived with Harold and Maggie. Saturday was three days away. Sandra didn't come to school any of those days and she only sent short responses to my texts saying that she wasn't at school because she wasn't feeling well but that she would be at the funeral on Saturday.

Harold and Maggie offered to go with me to the funeral. I said that they could drive me because it was being held at some funeral home that would have taken me two hours on the TTC to get to. But I didn't want them to go in with me. I told them that I wanted to be with my friends from work. Maggie said that they understood. "We'll just go to the coffee shop and you call us when you are ready to go home."

The funeral home was in a kind of strip mall. There was a dollar store across the street and a mattress store in the same plaza. To get to the room where Carly's funeral was being held I went down a hallway with a deep red carpet. At the door of the room was a stand with a picture of Carly and her name: Carly Samson 1997 – 2015. She looked a little younger in the picture. It must have been taken in the winter because she was wearing a white sweater and a green scarf. Behind her you could see a small house and a tree with no leaves. There was a little bit of snow on the ground. Carly was laughing in the picture. She looked really happy. I wished I had known her when she looked like that.

The room where the funeral was being held was small. About the size of a classroom. There were about twenty-five chairs set up. I went in and was relieved to see Tomasz, Philippe, Francois and a few other people from the restaurant already sitting down. I went straight over to them. On the other side of the room were a few people I assumed were Carly's friends from school. There were maybe twelve people. A couple of groups of three or four and one larger group of five. Most of them were looking at their phones. Sandra wasn't there yet. The only other people in the room were Detective Aquino and the cop from the TV with the crooked nose and acne scars. A few chairs at the front of the room had been roped off. There was a table set up at the front of the room with another copy of the picture of

Carly with the white sweater, an urn which I assumed held her ashes, a guest book and an arrangement of pink and white roses with a banner across which said "Our Darling Carly". There was one guy sitting next to Tomasz who I didn't recognize.

"This is Shakil," Tomasz introduced us. Shakil was immaculately groomed with beautiful, smooth brown skin and delicate hands with long fingers. He offered one of the delicate hands and said hello. This was obviously Tomasz's boyfriend. I stole a look at Tomasz and could see a half smile and a faint blush play on his face.

Everyone sat quietly. After about ten minutes a funeral home employee came in to announce that the service was about to begin and told us that she would be asking everyone to stand when the family entered. The funeral employee left and just then Sandra came in. She was wearing sunglasses and red lipstick. Tomasz leaned over and whispered in my ear, "why is Sandra dressed like a spy?" I couldn't help myself. I laughed out loud. Everyone looked at me. I just made an "I'm sorry" gesture and looked at my feet. Sandra came over and sat in the row behind us. I turned to say hi but she just looked past me towards the door of the room.

The funeral home employee came back and asked us all to stand. Carly's family came in. First was a middle-aged woman that I assumed was her mom, she had Carly's red hair, freckles and slender body type. She looked like she hadn't slept in days and her progress from the door of the room to her seat was wobbly. I doubt she would have made it if not for another woman, about the same age, who was helping her. This woman was more substantial in size than Carly's mom and she had a determined look on her face. I figured she must be a friend or maybe a sister who was there to support Carly's mom. After the two women came Brian. Even though I had only seen him that once on the street, the young man who came through the door could only have been Carly's brother. His face showed no emotion, but his energy was so angry I could feel it from the other side of the room. I heard Sandra draw in her breath and murmur, "un-fucking-believable". I didn't turn around. I fixed my eye on the flowers at the front of the room.

After Brian came an older man in a suit who was carrying a book and a black leather folder. The funeral home employee stood at the front, thanked everyone for coming, told us we could sit down, and introduced the man in the suit as Reverend Forsythe. He would be leading the funeral service. I found it hard to pay attention to what Reverend Forsythe was saying. He read something from the book he was carrying, which turned out to be the Bible, and then a prepared speech which he took out of the folder. He had obviously never met Carly and was just going through the motions. Eventually he invited Carly's aunt to say a few words. This was the woman who had come in with Carly's mom.

She still had the same determined look on her face that I had noticed when they came in. She had prepared a speech too, but at least she had known Carly. She talked about family camping trips and how Carly had loved to roast marshmallows on the campfire. I pictured her picking perfectly roasted marshmallows off a stick with her acrylic nails. Maybe she didn't have them back then, but I couldn't think of Carly without the nails.

Carly's aunt held it together really well through her whole speech. Just at the end she folded up her paper and turned to the picture of Carly beside the urn. "I'm so sorry Carly that we weren't there to protect you. We're going to miss you so much." Only then did her voice crack and she started to cry. Other people were crying too. I felt sad, but I didn't cry. The tears wouldn't come.

The whole thing took less than half an hour. People went to shake hands with the mother and aunt. Brian left the room as soon as the funeral home employee said that the service was over and asked people to sign the guest book. I was relieved that

I wouldn't have to shake hands with him. Carly's mom just sat and whispered thanks as people went up to her. The aunt had regained her composure and would look people in the eye and ask them how they knew Carly and thank them for coming. I thought she seemed like a really nice person. She reminded me of Maggie.

Sandra went out before us and I thought she would be gone by the time I got outside. She was still there. She had lit a cigarette and was standing to the side of the door when I came out. I couldn't ignore her. I decided I would behave as if nothing was wrong between us.

"Brutal, eh?" I hugged my jacket around me although it wasn't cold out.

Sandra took a drag of her cigarette and blew smoke out in exasperation. She grabbed me by the arm and led me across the parking lot, away from the building and the other funeral-goers who were still milling around outside. We were standing in front of the mattress store, far enough away that the others wouldn't be able to hear us. Sandra was flushed with anger. "I don't understand how those cops could just sit there with him in the room pretending to be the grieving brother when he fucking killed her!" In spite of her angry indignation, there was just the slightest lack of confidence in Sandra's voice. I couldn't go along. "But Sandra, we don't know that for sure. He wouldn't come to her funeral if he killed her, would he?"

"That's just what he wants people to think!"

I wanted to say that we should leave it up to the cops to figure out what had happened, but I knew that would make Sandra mad. I didn't need to say anything. She could tell by the fact that I wasn't agreeing with her that I doubted what she was saying.

"You know what your problem is, Frida?" Sandra pointed at my chest while still holding her cigarette so that I got a waft of smoke in my face as she told me off. "You and Tomasz, and the news, and the fucking cops, you are all the same. You are all prejudiced against Michal and Amir just because they are Albanians. Not all immigrants are crooks you know! Michal was right. He told me that no one would trust him because he's an immigrant. That's why he's not here. His heart is breaking, you know?! Did you ever think of that? Carly was his girlfriend. He loved her."

I was speechless. Sandra was right, I hadn't thought about the possibility of Michal's heart being broken over Carly's death. Even now, although Sandra was so adamant, when I thought about Michal and Carly I just couldn't picture him as broken-hearted. Maybe I am prejudiced, I thought to myself. Maybe I am not being fair to Michal.

Sandra flicked her cigarette away, "I gotta go. I'm meeting Amir later."

"Are you coming back to school next week?" I tried for a normal tone.

Sandra sighed. When she replied her voice was cold. "I don't know, Frida. Don't worry about me. See you around." She walked away.

Now my tears came. I knew she wouldn't be back at school the following week and I was right. What I didn't know was that it would be two and a half years before I saw her again.

VAKAROVSKY

Vakarovsky told me to come for extra help at lunch time. My first math test had not gone well. I realized that since grade seven I had been studying for math tests with Sandra. She always asked me to explain everything to her over and over again until she got it. Turns out this had been helpful preparation for tests, not just for her. This time, since Sandra hadn't been back at school and I didn't have anyone else to study with I just assumed that I knew the stuff and went into the test without really studying. I didn't fail, but Vakarovsky knew that I could do better.

When I went to the classroom at lunchtime, Ms. Johnston, the vice principal, was there talking to Mr. Vakarovsky. I waited outside the classroom. I wasn't trying to listen in, but Ms. Johnston had a loud voice and she was doing most of the talking. I wondered if Vakarovsky was in trouble. Ms. Johnston was getting ready to leave. She gathered up her lanyard with a bunch of keys attached and her walkie talkie. "It doesn't have to be sports. Could be chess or something. Give it some thought." I looked at my phone so that I wouldn't make eye contact with her as she left. Vakarovsky looked annoyed when I went in.

"Yes, Frida? What is it?"

"You told me to come for extra help at lunch. It's lunch now." I didn't think he was annoyed with me, he did tend to forget things.

"Oh yes, of course. Good. Take out the test, you will see that you made foolish errors." Showing me the mistakes I had made and making me do the questions again cheered him up. "Good! Now you see." He leaned back in his chair and put his hands behind his head with a satisfied smile.

"I heard you talking with Ms. Johnston. What was that about?" I had nobody to eat lunch with, so I figured that I may as well chat with Vakarovsky.

"Johnston? Is same thing every year. Teachers should sponsor some extra-curricular activity." He said "extra-curricular" like it was a disease.

"And you don't want to do that?"

"I am math teacher, not basketball coach."

"I heard her suggest chess. Would you want to start up a chess club?"

"Chess?" Vakarovsky looked bored with this idea. "Do you like to play chess, Frida?"

"No, sorry. I don't know how to play."

"It's alright. I don't like chess that much. What do you like to do aside from math?" I had to smile at this, but I didn't argue with his assumption that I liked to do math.

"I like to garden." This seemed to surprise him.

"Garden? With flowers?"

"Yes. And vegetables." This seemed to get his wheels turning. After searching for a moment through the chaos of books and papers on his desk he found a blank piece of paper. Further searching in his desk drawer produced a black marker.

He wrote at the top of the paper: "Gardening Club" then he drew five horizontal lines down the centre of the page. It was a sign-up sheet. On the first line he wrote "Frida".

"Congratulations. You are founding member of the gardening club."

"I don't know, Mr. Vakarovsky, I'm not much of a club person."

"Don't worry. Will not be much of a club. Soon snow will fall. No gardening. First meeting is tomorrow after school." He took the sign-up sheet for the gardening club and taped it to the board beside the door. That was to be the full extent of publicity for the gardening club.

I wondered what Vakarovsky had in mind for the gardening club. Pure curiosity led me to go to his classroom after school the next day. I wasn't expecting much. True to form, Vakarovsky had forgotten about gardening club, but I reminded him and he didn't seem too unhappy. "Okay, Frida. Let's go to get tools."

Vakarovsky led the way to a far corner of the school basement. The only classrooms that were down there were metal shop and wood working. There was a particular mix of smells, like a garage filled with teenaged boys. I felt completely out of place, so I just kept my head down and followed Vakarovsky. Eventually we arrived at a metal door with "Maintenance" written on it. Vakarovsky knocked. A youngish man with dark hair in a blue school-board shirt and blue work pants opened the door. He broke into a smile when he saw Vakarovsky and the two them immediately started speaking Russian. After a minute, Vakarovsky gestured towards me. "This is Frida. President of the Gardening Club. Frida, this is Yuri. He was my student some years ago."

Yuri smiled at me. "Is this guy your math teacher?" I nodded. "Lucky you! He's the best teacher. He helped me a lot."

"Okay. Enough chit chat." Vakarovksy interrupted. I wondered if he was embarrassed. "Time to garden!"

Yuri brought us into the store room down the hall and found us two shovels and two pairs of work gloves. Vakarovsky thanked him and after a short conversation in Russian, Yuri retrieved a key from the caretaker's office which he gave to Vakarovsky. We then went up a back staircase and down another hallway that I had never seen before. I started to wonder how many areas of the school there were that I was not familiar with. We arrived at a wall of windows that looked out onto a small courtyard. One of the windows was a metal-framed door that led out into the courtyard. Using the key that Yuri had given him, Vakarovsky unlocked the door and giving it a little push (it was clear that the door had not been opened in some time) he opened it and we stepped into the courtyard.

It was a space about the size of a large classroom. Three sides were windowed walls like the one with the door we had just come through and the fourth wall was brick. The courtyard was overgrown with shrubs and weeds. There were a lot of food wrappers and other garbage along one of the windowed sides. I could see that that side was where the cafeteria was. Some of the cafeteria windows opened onto the courtyard and obviously students had thrown their garbage out the windows. I had only been in the cafeteria to pick up my timetable and I had never noticed that the windows overlooked a courtyard.

"It's not beautiful, but there is a section in the middle that gets good sunlight and is protected from the wind. Good for garden." Vakarosvky was as energized as when he was doing equations on the white board. Without further comment he put on the gloves and started digging at a patch of ground in the middle of the courtyard that had lots of weeds, but no shrubs. Vakarovksy was an efficient digger. He would loosen the clumps of weeds, pull them out with a swift tug and then continue digging. He was totally absorbed in his work and before I could think of a way to get out of this he had cleared a four foot section. Aside from the gloves, he looked just as he did in math class. Same rumpled brown trousers and rumpled shirt with an old brown cardigan. He wore old leather dress shoes, also brown. Well, I reasoned to myself, at least he's colour coordinated with the dirt.

"Come on, Frida! Dig! Growing season is short."

"What are we going to grow now, Mr. Vakarovsky? It's almost October." I had started digging now too although I was nowhere near as efficient as Vakarovsky.

"No problem. We grow spinach, lettuce, radish. Very nice salad. You come again tomorrow and we will plant seeds."

I knew he was right. Lionel's mom had explained spring and fall crops versus summer crops. Thinking of Lionel and the allotment garden brought a pang. I was glad to have the digging to concentrate on so that I wouldn't start crying in front of Vakarovsky. We worked almost an hour in silence. It was long enough to prepare a decent-sized bed. We stood back and leaned on our shovels to survey our work. The weeds we had pulled were all piled up in a corner. "Yuri will collect them later," Vakarovsky told me.

"You didn't tell me that you knew how to garden, Mr. Vakarovsky. You have obviously done this before." I thought that I hadn't done too badly. Vakarovsky had nodded approvingly when I used the shovel to cut a sharp edge to the plot.

"My grandmother had a small garden back in Russia. I would always go to help her with the big jobs. She was very strong, she could have done everything alone, but I think she liked to have me there and I liked to think I was helping her." I tried to picture a young Vakarovsky helping his grandmother in the garden, but all my mind could conjure up was a small kid dressed in brown dress pants and shoes, a crumpled shirt and a brown cardigan. The picture made me smile, but I didn't want Vakarovsky to think I was laughing at him so I made a fuss of getting out my phone to take a picture of our work.

I realized, as I looked at the picture of a patch of dirt, that nobody but a gardener would appreciate the image and the work it represented. Without giving myself time to change my mind I sent the picture to Lionel with the caption "started a gardening club at school". As soon as I pressed send I put my phone away and swore to myself that I wouldn't look at it again until I got home from school. I tried not to think about Lionel getting the message, tried not to think about what his reaction would be. Vakarovsky and I left the courtyard, locked the door, returned the key to Yuri and went home.

With superhuman self-control I did not look at my phone until I got inside the house, dropped my bag and went up to my room. There was a message. I took a deep breath and touched the envelope icon. It was from Lionel. A thumbs up emoji. Could have been worse, I reasoned. He could have just not replied. But this was almost as bad. I mean, how do you respond to a thumbs up emoji? I pondered for a while, but I couldn't decide on the right response. I didn't want to appear desperate. Already the pathetic picture of a patch of dirt was bad enough. No, I decided I would just leave it. Maybe I could send some pictures of the seeds when they started to sprout. Satisfied with this plan, I went downstairs to see if I could find a snack.

I didn't know if Vakarovsky would bring seeds for planting. I had a bunch of seed packets that people from the allotment garden had given me. Some were commercial packets like you would get at the garden centre and others were homemade packets with handwritten notes giving the type of seed and the year they were harvested. I was keen to show Vakarovsky the seeds, but he wasn't in class period one. We had a supply teacher who had no idea why Vakarovsky wasn't there, or if she did know, she wouldn't tell us.

I was disappointed. I had been looking forward to getting those seeds in the ground. I wondered if I could get Yuri to let me into the courtyard. After school, I fought back back my anxiety about going down that weird hallway to the caretaker's office. I put my hood up and tried to walk as invisibly as possible. There were a few boys in the hallway, but they didn't give me a second glance. I knocked on the door. It was a heavy metal door, and my first attempt at knocking was so soft that Yuri would have needed supersonic hearing to notice it.

I stood for a minute trying to decide if I should give up or knock again. Another group of boys were coming in my direction. It was now or never. I summoned my courage and knocked hard with the side of my fist. This had the desired result. Yuri opened the door. He looked perplexed at first, but then he recognized me. "Oh hi! The gardening club president. You did a good job yesterday. I saw the plot you prepared." Yuri leaned his arm against the door frame.

Before I lost my nerve I asked, "Do you think you could let me into the courtyard to plant these seeds?" I dug the seed packets out of my backpack and showed them to Yuri. "Mr. Vakarovsky is not here today and I really want to get them in the ground before the weekend."

Yuri shook his head. "No can do. You need a teacher to supervise any after school activities. Those look like good seeds though. Maybe you can find another teacher to help you out."

"That's okay. I'll just wait until Vakarovsky is back." I put the seed packets back in my back pack.

"It might be a while, though, eh?" Yuri said.

"What do you mean?"

"You don't know?" Yuri brought his right arm down from the door frame and crossed it over his left arm.

"Know what?"

"Vakarovsky is in the hospital. He had a heart attack last night."

I couldn't believe this. Vakarovsky had never been sick. He had hardly missed any classes the entire time we had him as a teacher. "Oh shit. Is he okay?"

"I don't know too much." Yuri could see that I was freaking out. He put his hand on my shoulder. "Don't worry. He's a tough old bird. He'll pull through."

I thanked him and left as quickly as I could. The entire way home all I could think of was that I had done this. If it hadn't have been for me telling him that I liked gardening he wouldn't have gotten the shovels from Yuri and done all that work. I should have told him to let me do it. I felt awful.

When I got home the house was empty. I sat for a minute at the dining room table just feeling miserable. I had no one to talk to. After a few minutes, I got up and went to the cupboard where Harold kept his secret bottle of booze. I poured some into a glass and took a sip. The burning sensation I remembered from the night of the shooting was there again. Soon, I knew, the warmth would come. I drank another sip and another, until my mouth felt numb and the thoughts whirling in my head slowed down.

I put away the bottle. I washed the glass carefully and went up to my room.

SHOPPING TRIP
AND LINE-UP

—————— ı|ı| ——————

Vakarovsky went into hospital at the end of September. For a few days we had different supply teachers until they found someone who would take over the class. They found a young, pretty teacher who was very sweet and used coloured markers to do equations on the white board. Most of the class seemed to like her, but I couldn't forgive her for not being Vakarovsky.

I went through my days on auto-pilot. I felt like I was inside a glass box, but the glass wasn't clear, it was foggy or tinted or something. I could see and hear what was going on, but it didn't really register. I must have looked clued out. People at school mostly ignored me. Harold was working long hours and was super stressed about deadlines for the Eglinton Crosstown so he didn't really have much time or energy for me. Maggie tried making me my favourite food, she offered to take me to the movies, she brought home multiple self-help books from the library. I just felt numb and exhausted all the time. As soon as I got home from school, I would lie down and sleep. Sometimes I couldn't even wake up for dinner, and I would sleep straight through to morning.

One Saturday Maggie brought me a cup of tea to my room. She sat on the edge of the bed while I drank the tea. She had taken a shower earlier in the morning and I could could smell the herby, floral shampoo that she used.

"What if we go shopping today?" Maggie refolded a stack of my laundry that she had already folded the day before. I knew that she wished she could straighten up whatever was going on in my head as easily as she could fold t-shirts and jeans into a symmetrical pile. I wished that too; I wanted to feel better. The hot tea and the Maggie's shampoo smell were pleasant and I wanted to show her that I was trying, so I agreed to go shopping.

It was like moving through molasses to get dressed and brush my teeth and hair. I didn't have much appetite, but I ate a banana.

We always took the subway downtown to go shopping because parking was expensive and the traffic bad. Being on the subway with Maggie felt strange. Ever since starting work at Bouillabaisse I would ride the subway either with Sandra or by myself. I felt younger being with Maggie, but I also felt older because, unlike when we had ridden the subway together for shopping excursions in the past, I was more comfortable out in the world. I didn't rely on Maggie for security. I knew the subway, I knew how to choose my seat and avoid potential uncomfortable encounters. I hadn't gone anywhere except school since Carly's funeral, and it felt good to be out. As the train came above ground just north of Bloor, I started to feel energized. I could see the buildings and streets of the city centre and I anticipated the crush of people that we would join when we got off at Queen Street to go to the Eaton Centre.

Instinctively I tucked my bag under my arm and put on my "don't mess with me" face. I could see Maggie looking at me, but I felt good. I wanted to take her arm because she looked a little soft in her beige jacket and silk scarf.

The energy buzz kept going for about an hour. We bought some shoes and a pair of jeans. My eyes started to burn and the noise of the mall was pounding in my ears. Maggie could see I was fading. "Let's get a snack."

We went to the food court. There was a cafe-style place with nice coffee, sandwiches and pastries. There were a few people in line. I was looking at the menu board when I heard someone impatiently explaining the difference between a latte and a cappuccino to an older woman in a red coat and large earrings. "Well, I want a latte," she was saying, "but with lots of foam. I like the foam." I really wanted to see the reaction of the barista. When I looked behind the counter, my jaw dropped. It was Tomasz. He sighed in exasperation at the red coat woman and rolled his eyes. That's when he saw me.

"Frida!" His face lit up and he totally ignored the red coat woman to wave me over. "What are you doing here?"

Seeing Tomasz totally revived my energy. I realized how much I had missed the restaurant. I wanted to jump behind the counter and work the espresso machine.

Tomasz told his tiny blond co-worker to help the red coat lady and got coffee and pastries for me and Maggie. He charmed Maggie by complimenting her scarf. He told us that he couldn't take a break to sit with us but that he wasn't working the next day if I wanted to meet for brunch.

Maggie was quiet as we walked back through the mall. She tried for a light tone, "Tomasz seems nice."

"Oh yeah! He taught me everything at Bouillabaisse. If it wasn't for him I never would have made it."

Maggie nodded and smiled. "How old is he?"

"Tomasz? I don't know, maybe twenty? He came from Poland five years ago." It occurred to me that Maggie may have gotten the wrong idea. I needed to set her straight. "Don't get any ideas. He's gay."

"What ideas? I don't have ideas. That's fine that he's gay. I'm just glad you have a friend."

I hadn't told Maggie about the argument with Sandra, but obviously she noticed that I never went out anymore and Sandra's name never came up. I knew that Maggie knew and I was glad that she hadn't asked me about it. Maggie patted my arm and we left the mall together.

When we got home, Harold was waiting for us. He shifted his weight from one foot to the other and didn't seem to know where to put his hands. Maggie put down the shopping bags. "What is it, Harold? What happened?"

Harold cleared his throat. "That police detective called."

"Detective Aquino?" I asked.

"That's the one." Harold started walking down the hall towards the kitchen. For a second I thought nervously about the bottle of rye whiskey. What if he went to look for it now and noticed there was some missing? Harold didn't go to get the rye whiskey. He stopped beside the dining table and rested his hand on the back of one of the chairs. "She wants Frida to go down to the station."

"Maggie sat unevenly in one of the other chairs. "Why? Why does Frida have to go down there again?"

"Detective Aquino said that they have made an arrest and they want Frida to help with the identification."

I felt hot all over and then suddenly cold. "Did they say who they had arrested?"

"No. I didn't ask, actually." Harold looked a little embarrassed, but I knew he would have been tongue-tied in such an unusual conversation.

"When are we supposed to go?" Maggie asked.

"As soon as possible, they said." I was glad that we could go right away. This way I didn't have time to get nervous.

We drove in silence to the police station. The cop at the front desk called for someone to come take us into a small room in the station where we waited about twenty minutes before Detective Aquino came in. Just before entering the room, she stood talking to another cop in the hallway about the coffee machine which was not working and Detective Aquino was telling the other cop what he should do to get it working again. Hearing this everyday conversation made me relax a little. If they could talk about coffee machines then things must be under control.

Detective Aquino came in and introduced herself to Maggie, said hello to me and Harold and thanked them for bringing me so promptly. Harold and Maggie sat side by side and as Detective Aquino talked to them they held hands and nodded at what she was saying. Detective Aquino asked how I had been coping. Maggie looked at me, "Frida has been trying to get back to her life and put all this behind her." I was grateful that she didn't tell Detective Aquino about the excessive sleeping and falling out with Sandra. I was sitting on the other side of the room. Initially I had been grateful that Detective Aquino had spoken to Harold and Maggie first. But I didn't want her to think I was a useless basket-case, so I spoke up now.

"I was pretty messed up for a few days after, but I'm okay now. I am ready to do whatever you need."

Detective Aquino smiled a little and reoriented her sitting position so that she was talking to me.

"We are very grateful, Frida. You can really help us with this case and make sure whoever did this to Carly is punished."

I straightened my back and tried to put on my most mature voice. "Who did it? I mean, who did you arrest?"

"We have arrested a young man from Montreal. We had some information that he had been in Toronto at the time of the shooting. He's someone who is known to Montreal police. He's involved in a drug-dealing operation there."

Detective Aquino paused to let this information sink in. Harold and Maggie looked at me to see my reaction. I had to ask. "So it wasn't Brian? It wasn't Carly's brother who shot her?"

"At this time we don't believe Brian was involved in the shooting."

"But why would his guy from Montreal want to shoot Carly?"

"We believe that the intended target of the shooting was not Carly. It looks like she was in the wrong place at the wrong time."

"Was he trying to kill Michal?"

Detective Aquino tilted her head to one side as if to see me at a different angle. Harold and Maggie were silent, but I could sense their surprise. Detective Aquino didn't look surprised, I doubt anything was surprising to her, but she did lean a little toward me and looked right into my eyes. "Why would you think that, Frida?"

I cycled through my mind the things Tomasz had said about Michal, images of Carly and Michal kissing in the alleyway, and Sandra saying that the cops were prejudiced against Michal.

"Well, Carly was standing right by the table where Michal was sitting. So if he was aiming for Michal he might have hit Carly instead." I thought that I sounded very rational.

Detective Aquino nodded. "That's true. She was standing right next to his table. We are not finished our investigation, but right now we are trying to make sure we have the right person in custody for the shooting. Frida, are you ready to do an identification for us?"

Howard spoke up. "Detective Aquino, Frida never saw the shooter's face. How will she be able to help you?"

"When we arrested the suspect, he had a pair of black jeans and black boots in his possession. We're going to see if Frida recognizes them. She won't be asked to look at anyone's face."

Maggie stood up and came over to me. "What do you think, Frida? Do you want to try?"

I felt a little silly. Would I really be able to identify a pair of boots? I thought of Sandra. If it had been her instead of me under that table, she would have lunged at the shooter to prevent him from leaving, or at least she would have gotten a good look at him. Well, Sandra wasn't here now, I thought to myself. I had to play the part that I had been given.

"I'm ready. I'll do my best."

Detective Aquino stood up. "Great. Give us a few minutes to organize the line up. You're going to see four different legs in jeans and boots. Take your time and see if one looks familiar from the night of the shooting."

Harold, Maggie and I were left alone in the small room while detective Aquino went to organize the line up. Maggie came to sit beside me and put her arm around my shoulder. I wanted to just rest my head on her chest and cry and say that I couldn't do it, but I also wanted to be brave, do what was needed, maybe play a part in catching the person who had done this to Carly. Maggie was stroking my arm gently, "Frida, did you know this Michal person?" I pulled away from her a little.

"Not that well. He was Carly's boyfriend."

Maggie looked at Harold. She hoped he would know the right thing to do or say. He looked blank, but he had picked up on Maggie's unspoken plea for help. "Well Frida, just make sure you tell the police everything you know. Maybe something you don't think is important is actually a vital piece of information."

"I already told them everything I know. He was a customer at the restaurant and he was dating Carly."

Maggie folded her arms the way she would when she told me to clean my room or do the dishes. "I just hope you are telling us and the police everything. You never know what these kind of people are mixed up in. You have to be careful."

"What do you mean 'these kind of people'? Just because he's an immigrant doesn't mean he's a bad person!" I heard myself talking in Sandra's words but I couldn't match her indignation. I wasn't at all sure whether Michal was a good person or not.

"We know that Frida." Harold ran his hand across his balding head. I imagined that he was thinking of that bottle of rye whiskey.

Detective Aquino came back to the room just then. The little bit of anger this exchange with Harold and Maggie had generated gave me the push I needed to hold my head up and give a firm nod when Detective Aquino asked "Ready?"

They had set up a room with a table coved with a tablecloth that hung down over the edges of the table just like the ones at Bouillabaisse. In fact I thought it could have been a table and tablecloth from the restaurant that they had brought to the station. Beyond the table was a black curtained panel that divided the space. Detective Aquino explained that they wanted to recreate my position in the restaurant on the night of the shooting so that I would have a better chance of recognizing the legs with boots. "We will have four different people walk in through the door at the end of the room. They won't be able to see you, and you will only be able to see what you saw on the night of the shooting.

There were three other people in the room as well. Detective Aquino explained that they were the Crown Attorney, the lawyer for the person who had been arrested and her partner, the cop with the bad skin who had gone on TV after the shooting. I said that I understood and I went over to the table. I crouched down like I had done that night and I said I was ready. My heart was pounding, but I knew I had to go through with it now.

Detective Aquino called for the first person to come through the door. The door opened and someone came through with clomping steps. The boots were black with no laces, and the legs wore black jeans, but this was definitely not the pair of legs and feet I had seen that night. The footsteps were too heavy, clumsy almost. The boots were scuffed and looked as though they had taken on the shape of the wearer's feet. The jeans weren't right either. They were too loose. I looked at Detective Aquino and shook my head. The two lawyers made notes in identical black notebooks.

The next three people were closer to being right. The third one was wrong because the jeans had a section at the bottom that was a slightly different colour, as if they had been rolled up for a while and then let down so that the section that had been rolled up was not as faded as the rest of the leg.

Number two and number four were very similar. The boots were right. Not scuffed, but not too new. The jeans were the right fit and colour. On number two the hem of the jeans sat slightly lower than on number four. I asked if I could see number two again. Detective Aquino called for number two. I closed my eyes and tried to picture the night of the shooting. The rush of wind and rain as the door opened. The bread crumbs on the floor. I tried to see the boots again. I saw them come in. Stop. The sound of the shots. I saw Carly crumple to the floor. I turned back to look at the feet again. Now, crouching under the table at the police station, my legs were shaking and I was sweating with anxiety. But I could picture those feet walking out the door. The back of the jeans were low, they were a slightly darker colour because they were wet. It was raining and the bottom of the jeans had gotten wet. I peered out from under the table to look at Detective Aquino. She looked at me questioningly.

"It's number two."

"You're sure?"

"Yes."

"Okay Frida, you can come out from under there now."

I stood up and felt light-headed for a minute. Detective Aquino reached out to steady me. "You okay?"

I looked at her and I could tell by her expression that I had identified the right person. "I'm fine."

I was riding high as we came out of the police station. I felt like I had done really well with the identification and when we got to the car, Maggie told me to ride up front with Harold. I felt like I had regained some control.

When we got home I ate a huge pasta dinner while Maggie watched with amazement. I went to bed early. I dreamed that Sandra was a police detective standing in front of Bouillabaisse on a rainy summer night taking notes in a black notebook. Periodically she would look up from her notebook, nod and smile knowingly.

The next day I was still feeling energized and confident. I went down to the Danforth to meet Tomasz for brunch. He had texted me while I was asleep with the name of the place and the meeting time. It was a small cafe where you would go up to the counter to order your food and coffee and then they would bring it to your table. When I arrived Tomasz and Shakil were already sitting at a table. Tomasz waved me over when he saw me and stood to give me a hug. The cafe was warm and full of the delicious aromas of coffee, baked goods and breakfast food. Most of the tables were full: families with kids, older couples, groups of young people. Everyone seemed relaxed and happy and it was quite noisy with people talking and dishes clattering. It was the clattering dishes sound that reminded me of the restaurant and caused my heart to start beating quickly. I hadn't been in a restaurant since the shooting.

If Tomasz suspected that I was feeling anxious he didn't acknowledge it. "You remember Shakil?" I nodded at Tomasz's boyfriend who I remembered from Carly's funeral. He was just as well-groomed for Sunday brunch as he had been for Carly's funeral. He was wearing a beautiful cream-coloured sweater that set off his dark skin. He was truly beautiful and he made me feel at ease right away.

"Thank God you have arrived, Frida. Tomasz will not shut up about the espresso machine and how they need to adjust the steam valve or something." This made me laugh remembering Tomasz's obsessive relationship with the Gaggia at Bouillabaisse. We ordered food and coffee and sat chatting until most of the other tables had left. I complimented Shakil on his sweater. "Oh, thank you! I'm glad you like it." Shakil took the compliment without any fake modesty. He knew he was beautiful and there was no point in denying it. Tomasz sat beside him with an expression that said he could hardly believe his luck.

"Frida, you should come with us to Artemesia right now. I saw a jacket in the window on the way here that would suit you so well." Shakil went to the bathroom. Tomasz and I were getting ready to leave.

"You know that Shakil will give you a complete makeover if you let him. He is always trying to tell me what to wear and how to cut my hair, but I don't listen. He'll be so happy if you will take his advice." I could see how Tomasz would resist fashion and grooming advice. He wasn't a sloppy dresser; he was certainly neat and tidy as someone working in high end food service needed to be, but he would never wear a beautiful cream sweater.

I wanted to see what suggestions Shakil might make so I agreed to go to Artemesia which turned out to be a small clothing boutique a little further west on Danforth. The jacket that Shakil had seen in the window was something I never would have looked at for myself. We went in and Shakil asked to have it taken out of the window for me to try. The girl who was working there looked a bit doubtful, but Shakil was insistent.

He picked out a plain black top for me to put on underneath since the faded blue hoodie I had on was never going to work.

The jacket was made of a velvety corduroy type of fabric. It was cut quite slim but the collar and lapels were slightly large so that it looked like something from old Beatles footage. The jacket was green, and the buttons were a rich reddish brown, and the jacket was lined with a similar colour of satin.

I felt nervous trying it on, but Shakil took charge. He put it on me, did up a few of the buttons, adjusted the collar and then tilted his head to examine me. He smiled. "I knew it would work."

I looked at myself in the shop mirror. I was still Frida, just more interesting. My eyes looked different, less of a nondescript brown, more rich somehow. The jacket looked as though it had been made for me. I was so thin and flat-chested that most tops and jackets hung badly on me, but this was was perfect and the cut, just below the hips, make me look as though I might have some curve.

I looked at Shakil and I thought I might cry. I didn't. I just hugged him and bought the jacket. The salesgirl seemed almost jealous. "That jacket looks great on you." I knew it was true and I wore it home. I put my blue hoodie in the bag from the store. I felt like I was walking on air with my new jacket, Tomasz and Shakil beside me, chatting away. We said goodbye at Pape and Danforth. They were going to do more shopping, and I was heading home. I crossed Danforth to head towards the subway entrance. Ahead of me I noticed someone crossing Pape in the other direction, just north of the lights, before the subway entrance. He was moving nervously, looking all around him, not just at cars but at the pedestrians on the sidewalk. It wasn't clear if he was looking for someone he wanted to see or for someone he didn't want to see. My guess was the latter. He was focused on crossing the road against the lights, so I thought he hadn't noticed me, but I saw who it was and the sight of that person made my heart come into my throat. It was Amir.

Immediately I wondered if Sandra was with him or maybe he was going to meet her. For a split second I wanted to call out to him, but I didn't. I tried to play cool and keep walking. Just as I neared the station I stopped to look at my phone. As casually as I could, I turned back to face the direction I had come to see if I could see where Amir had gone. He was on the other side of the street. He had seen me. He was standing awkwardly in the middle of the sidewalk staring at me. Our eyes met and I thought I saw a moment of fear or anxiety cross his face, as though I had caught him doing something he shouldn't have been doing. This made me feel strange and I didn't know what to do, so I just turned away and went into Pape station. I was shaken up. My green jacket confidence, while not totally destroyed, had been weakened. As the train travelled north I knew that the whiskey bottle was going to get a visit when I got home and that idea was a comfort.

CALLIOPE

The green jacket wasn't the only magic Shakil worked on me. The following weekend, Tomasz invited me to go with them to a dance club called Calliope in Boytown. I had never been to a dance club and I didn't know much about Boytown, but I trusted Tomasz and Shakil and I had nothing else to do, so I agreed. "Come to our place early so Shakil can help you get ready."

"Getting ready" involved Shakil doing my hair, my makeup and my outfit. He had bags of clothing and shoes in the bedroom closet and he expertly went through the whole selection, pausing briefly to hold a top up to me or check my shoe size. The silver high heels he chose ended up being a bit small, but I didn't want to complain, and there was no denying they went well with the rest of the outfit he had chosen: a very short electric blue skirt and a clingy patterned top with sequins. I felt nervous and excited about going out dressed like that, but Shakil and Tomasz were exuberant in their praises.

We started drinking some sort of cocktail that Tomasz mixed. It was nothing like Harold's whiskey, it didn't burn going down, and although it didn't have the same immediate numbing effect, it did make me feel happy and confident and it was tasty so I kept drinking. When we got into the Uber to go the club I started singing loudly along with the Ariana Grande song that was playing. Tomasz and Shakil laughed and sang along too. The Uber driver seemed mildly annoyed, but we didn't care.

We arrived at Calliope and didn't wait in line because Tomasz knew the bouncer. "I was bartender at the club where he worked before." The club was crowded. The weather had started to get cooler, especially in the evenings and coming into the heat and noise of the club from the brisk night air was a little overwhelming. The crowd was ninety-five percent gay men, each one more beautiful and gorgeously done up than the other. Shakil still stood out, but slightly less. Tomasz steered us directly to the bar, where, of course, he knew the bartender and he ordered us amazing blue cocktails that made me feel like I was drinking electricity.

We joined the pulsing crowd on the dance floor. Most people danced in pairs or small groups, but one dancer was in his own world. His torso was bare save for a tiny leather vest and I could see that he was glistening with sweat as he danced like he was possessed. His eyes were closed and his head was down, but his limbs and body moved perpetually, not really in time to the music, but following some internal rhythm that was clearly driving him. The other dancers were less intense. They danced with their eyes open, appraising or connecting with the people around them. I got separated from Tomasz and Shakil while watching the frenetic solo dancer. The music didn't let up and I started to feel strange. I made my way to the side of the club where there were some benches. Quite a few couples were enthusiastically making out there, but I was beyond caring. I just needed to sit down.

I squeezed myself next to a well-muscled blond guy who had another man draped over him. I closed my eyes and felt the room start to spin. I felt hot all over and my legs seemed to turn to rubber. I couldn't stop myself from sliding off the bench and onto the floor. It was darker on the floor, I realized and it felt a little cooler down there, so I just let myself go limp. How long I stayed like that I don't know, but eventually Tomasz and Shakil found me. They laughed and made me drink two glasses of water. I wondered how I looked. Tomasz and Shakil looked as perfect as when we had come in, just slightly flushed from dancing or drinking, or both.

Before calling an Uber for me they walked me around Boytown. I threw up in the bank parking lot at Church and Wellesley and Shakil wiped my face with some napkins he got from an all-night shawarma shop. They sent me back to North York with instructions to drink more water and take a Tylenol before going to sleep.

GOING TO THE PARK

I settled into my grade twelve year without Sandra. I hadn't heard from her. Tomasz and Shakil became my closest friends, but of course they weren't at school with me and it seemed that Vakarovsky wasn't coming back any time soon. This was how I discovered a group of fellow students I had never noticed before. I came within their orbit one day during a fire drill. I was in English class and the bell rang. Our English teacher wasn't too keen on rounding us up to count heads outside like they were supposed to do. She just scanned us briefly with her eyes while holding her attendance folder open and then went to gossip with the other English teachers while we all stood around waiting for the all clear.

I had been wearing my green jacket almost every day and I had it on that day so at least I wasn't cold like some of the girls who were in tiny tops. A few used this excuse to cuddle up to or borrow sweaters from boys and this made me smile and remember kissing Marc Andre on the cold Queen Street East rooftop.

I noticed three kids, a girl and two guys, walking away from the school, across the playing field towards the residential neighbourhood that abutted the school grounds. Whatever magnet had drawn them together pulled me too that day and I walked after them. I didn't call out but I wasn't trying to be subtle and when one of the guys stopped to light a cigarette I came close enough to make it obvious I was following them.

Vivian was the only one that I knew by name. She was a tiny, dark-haired girl who hardly spoke, but had a nice smile and wore an amazing assortment of silver rings on her small hands. Vivian had sat near me in social science glass the year before and although she never spoke in class, she seemed to be into the topics and when the teacher returned assignments or tests, I noticed she got really high marks. That was not the only thing that made me remember her. One day the teacher had been giving a lesson on Freud. Vivian got a really angry look on her face as the teacher was explaining Freud's psychosexual development theory and I heard her swearing under her breath "fucking misogynist!". I had to look up what a misogynist was, but I was impressed by her anger and it made me remember her.

"Hi Vivian. I see you guys are escaping the blaze." It was a little windy that day and the leaves were starting to come off the trees that lined the fence separating the school grounds from the residential neighbourhood. I can remember the leaves of those trees falling behind Vivian and the two guys as they stood to look at me. One guy was tall and thin with dark, shaggy hair and the beginnings of a beard. He wore a faded army jacket with a bunch of buttons for various bands and causes. The other guy was not as tall, but he carried more weight. The weight sat well on him, making him look strong rather than unfit. He was the one who had stopped to light a cigarette and he took a drag of it now as he sized me up.

Although both guys were physically larger, taller and bigger, than Vivian, she seemed to be in charge. After looking me over, they both looked at her to see whether she would give permission for me to join their group. I got the sense that the best thing I could do to gain acceptance was to just stand quietly and wait. I knew that they knew who I was. I still had a certain infamy from being witness to a shooting and obviously Sandra had disappeared, leaving me friendless.

Vivian smiled "Hey Frida. We're just going to the park. You know Alex and Andreas?" I nodded at tall, thin Andreas and heavy set Alex and we all continued walking together. The park Vivian mentioned was a very small patch of green space just on the other side of the school grounds fence. There was a walkway that connected the neighbourhood to the school grounds, but the shape of the grounds was a little irregular so there was this patch of green that wasn't anyone's yard, and wasn't part of the school grounds. It was a little overgrown with shrubs and full of leaves that had fallen from the many trees around, so it was secluded. There were plenty of cigarette butts around so it was obviously a place people came to hang out and smoke. I was amazed that I had never seen it before even though this was my fourth year at the school.

A fallen tree limb made a good bench for me and Vivian. Andreas took off his army jacket and sat on that. Alex didn't sit. He leaned up against a tree. From my vantage point, sitting on the tree limb, he looked very imposing. He had an intense way of looking at you when he was talking. I tried to maintain eye contact but it was difficult. I felt like he could see right through me. He was talking about American politics. He was happy about some of the results in the election, which I knew nothing about. I knew about the President, of course, and what a disaster he was and how our Prime Minister couldn't stand him. Alex had a whole other level of familiarity with the issues.

"It's the way he treats women that pisses me off." Vivian wasn't intimidated by Alex's pronouncements on Democratic control of the House of Representatives. She spoke more slowly than Alex. I wondered if she had a stutter or something because she paused for longer than normal before some words and I could tell that she was really concentrating on what she was saying. "Look how they had to cover up all the … allegations from that Playboy model. And look at the way he treats those families in the … immigration … detention centres. How can any human being … separate small children from their families?"

Alex and Andreas listened carefully to what she said. They nodded and murmured their agreement, but they didn't interrupt or get distracted while she was talking. I wished that I had something to say that would cause them to listen to me with the same attention.

Andreas didn't talk much. After Vivian finished what she was saying, he reached into the pocket of his army jacket and took out a bag of weed and some rolling papers. Alex took the lead again, this time switching to Ontario politics. "I can't believe that even seeing what is going on in the States people still voted in that wannabe with his 'buck a beer'. It's pure populism! Can't people see through that?" He was genuinely confused.

I didn't know what to say, but I couldn't stay quiet any longer or they would think I was an idiot.

"I guess people will vote for whoever talks about what is important to them. Maybe cheap beer is important to a lot of people."

Andreas had rolled and lit the joint and was passing it to me. I knew I had to take it without comment and I wasn't worried I would choke or anything. Even thought I had basically stopped smoking since leaving Bouillabaisse, I still knew how to inhale. I was glad to have an excuse to interrupt my speech on voting decisions because I had very little else to say.

Alex watched me inhale. He crouched down next to me to take the joint. I felt the warmth of his body and when his fingers touched mine in order for him to take the joint I felt a current pass through me. My cheeks grew warm. Alex stood up again and held the joint carefully while he looked off towards the houses in the neighbourhood just beyond the shrubs that shielded us from view. "You're right there, Frida. And that's just what the populists understand." He took another drag and passed the joint to Vivian who passed it back to Andreas without taking a drag. Alex continued. "They know that they can get votes by appealing to our basest instincts. That's why they play on our fears and go so big on 'law and order'." Alex stood like a politician giving a speech. "Don't worry, my fellow Ontarians! We will be hiring more police officers so you can all feel safe!"

We all laughed at Alex's stuffed shirt imitation. He could really pull it off. "Yeah, right!" I scoffed. "You can all feel safe unless you're a black guy talking to a white girl at the side of the road!"

Vivian, Andreas and Alex all looked at me expectantly. The wind picked up just then and blew a bunch of leaves over us. It seemed to get cold in that instant, the way it can in October. I stood up to shake the leaves off and move around for warmth. Alex came close to me to pluck a leaf from my hair. The heat and energy of him seemed to wash over me and I wanted him to put his arms around me. He didn't. Vivian's phone buzzed and she told us she had to go to pick up her little brother.

We walked back towards the school. Classes were going to be over soon, so we didn't go back inside. Vivian gave me a hug and whispered in my ear, "I'm glad you came to the park today." I was grateful that they had included me.

Alex and Andreas were going to walk over to the mall to get something to eat, and Vivian had to get a different bus than I did, so we said goodbye. I watched them walk away, Alex and Andreas in one direction and Vivian in another. I thought about what Sandra would say. What would she think of those three? I imagined that she would have monopolized the politics discussion. She would have introduced some idea or information that nobody else had. She would have dazzled and captivated all three of them, especially Alex. I could almost see Alex listening to her with rapt attention and then wrapping his arms around her to get closer to her.

Where was she? I wondered.

ALEX

Most weekends that fall I would go to Calliope with Tomasz and Shakil. I developed a persona that I would slip into as I drank Tomasz's sweet cocktails and allowed Shakil to dress and doll me up in their apartment before we would set off for the club. This persona was bubbly and fun. She would laugh loudly and sing and dance without self-consciousness. Shakil even had a name for her: Miss Flower Power. I didn't know anyone else at the club. They were interested in me only as a decorative piece. Shakil would primp and show off the latest clothes, hair and makeup he had me in and I had no responsibility but to drink, smile and laugh. It was a wonderful escape from the mounting pressure of grade twelve and Harold and Maggie's questions about what Universities I was applying to.

When I had to be Frida, at school and at home, I managed by drinking on my own and getting high with Alex, Andreas and Vivian. If Harold and Maggie suspected how much I was drinking, they never confronted me about it. I got Tomasz to buy me a bottle of Rye Whiskey like Harold's. I topped up his bottle to replace whatever I may have drank and I kept the rest hidden in my room. It was a comfort to know it was there, and after Harold and Maggie went to sleep, I would sip myself numb.

In mid-November Paul got a position with an engineering firm in Calgary and Harold and Maggie took time off work to fly out and help him get settled. They asked me if I wanted to come with them, but I said that I would be okay staying alone.

"We'll call you every day, Frida" Maggie reassured me. "Stay focussed on your classes, you'll have to do your university applications soon." Harold and Maggie had been telling me for the past couple of years not to worry about the cost of university, that they had enough saved up for me to go to any Canadian university. They didn't put any pressure to go into any particular program, but that I would go to University was a given.

I felt guilty because I had skipped all the university information sessions to go to the park with Alex, Andreas and Vivian. At first I had assumed that they were all applying to university and I had been all ready to go to the Western University information session when Vivian told me, "I still need five credits to graduate after this year." I must have looked confused when she told me this. "I missed a lot of school in grade nine and ten. I was really messed up and I got behind on my credits."

Alex, I discovered, had one primary goal: to escape from his parents, especially his father who was an executive at an investment firm downtown. Alex's family was super rich, Vivian had told me. He had always gone to private boarding school up until grade twelve when he insisted on going to a public school. His aunt was a teacher at our school and his parents reluctantly enrolled him thinking that his aunt would be able to keep an eye on him.

They didn't realize that an English teacher at a big public high school has very little time for anything beyond teaching their classes and marking huge stacks of papers. Alex's aunt would sometimes stop him in the hallway to check how he was doing, but she didn't watch him too closely. Alex was super smart and was acing all his classes without even trying. He had already decided that he was going to Concordia University in Montreal and had no need to attend information sessions.

Andreas had no plans to attend university. His parents owned a large Estonian bakery and as soon as he finished high school he would be going to work there full time. I was intrigued. I asked him about it one day while we were waiting for Vivian and Alex to get out of their history class. "Is that what you want to do? Work in your parents' bakery?"

"I don't mind." Andreas spoke very little.

I felt like I should encourage him to aim for something more. I remembered our guidance counsellor helping us choose potential careers by asking what our favourite classes were. I tried this tactic with Andreas. "What classes do you like best?"

"I don't really like any classes in school." Andreas was turning a little red. I should have stopped there, but I didn't.

"Come on. Which classes do you do best in? Math? English? Social science?" It dawned on me as I was asking this that I had never had a class with Andreas. Vivian had been in social science and Alex was in English with me. I was taking maths and sciences and Alex and Vivian were taking history and philosophy, so that made sense. But I had never had a class with Andreas, even though I was pretty sure that he had been at the school since grade nine, just like I had.

"When my family came from Estonia, it was difficult." Andreas looked at the floor. I wanted to tell him it was okay, he didn't need to explain anything to me, but I could see he had made up his mind to tell me. "I had trouble in school even in Estonia, but here it was worse. I learned to speak English, but my reading and writing were always so bad. The teachers would try to help me, but I couldn't learn." This was the most I had ever heard him speak and it was the first time I realized that he had a slight accent, sort of like Mr. Vakarovsky's, but not as strong.

"I didn't know, Andreas. I didn't even know you were Estonian."

"I think I am more Canadian than Estonian now." Andreas smiled shyly.

"I'm sure your parents will be glad to have you helping them in the bakery."

Luckily Alex and Vivian's class let out just then and Andreas and I were released from the awkwardness. Andreas and Vivian walked together down the hallway, Alex and I followed behind. They didn't talk as they walked, but you could tell they liked to be together. The hallway was busy with kids leaving class and going to their locker, and there was some jostling, but Andreas and Vivian bumped into one another as they walked more than would really be justified by the crowding in the hallway. When the grade nine basketball team came through the main foyer en masse, seemingly unaware of any other people in the space, Andreas positioned himself protectively between them and Vivian.

Alex and I did not jostle into one another as we walked down the hallway. Alex was holding forth about the Renaissance. He was disappointed in the lesson they had just had in history class and was anxious to ensure that I realized that "the Renaissance is an invented concept of Eurocentric historians." I listened to him, I loved to hear him talk, but a part of me was paying attention to Vivian and Andreas and willing him to put his arm around her or for Vivian to reach out and hold his hand.

It was getting too cold to sit in the little park for very long. "Couldn't we go to The Palace?" Vivian asked Alex. She called his house The Palace because it was so big.

"Too far, and the servants are always underfoot, you know." Alex had a British "lord of the manor" accent that he would put on when talking about his family or his boarding school. They weren't British but that was his act that he would put on. I figured it made it easier to make fun of them, make them into characters you would see in a movie rather than his actual family.

"We could go to my place." It occurred to me that this was perfect. Harold and Maggie were in Calgary. "The house is empty."

"Well, alright Frida!" Alex looked at me approvingly and I felt a bit weak in the knees.

I tried to play it cool. "It's no palace, but there might be some snacks."

Andreas and Vivian laughed at this but Alex looked a bit stung. Was it the palace reference, I wondered, or the snacks?

We caught the bus. It was crowded and Alex stood out. He didn't seem to know how to make himself smaller to take up only the minimal amount of space. Alex was a good size, but I had ridden the bus with enormous, tall guys who could just incline their heads, fold up their limbs and take no more space than an elderly Chinese lady. I realized that it wasn't so much the physical space that Alex took up, it was the space he took up with his personality. He was way too present on that bus. He looked at people with interest. He cleared his throat and launched into a tirade on transit underfunding. I didn't know how to stop him. Andreas and Vivian had slipped through to the back of the bus and were enjoying the excuse to stand close together and fall into one another with every lurch and turn of the bus. Thankfully, the bus ride was not too long and I could sense the entire ridership's relief when I told Alex, "We're the next stop."

No friends had been to my house since Sandra, and I was anxious about having Vivian, Andreas and Alex see me in my home. I remembered going to the basement where Sandra lived when I first met her. At that time I had no way to understand what it meant that Sandra lived in that crummy apartment. But I knew that Vivian, Andreas and Alex would understand a lot about me when they saw Harold and Maggie's neat little suburban house. I wasn't ashamed of Harold and Maggie. There was nothing wrong with the house, but I knew that once they saw my house they would fill out certain blanks in their mental description of me. I wasn't sure whether this understanding would lead them to think better or worse of me, but we were here now and I opened the front door.

Vivian and Alex went straight to the kitchen and looked out the window into the back yard. "Is that your garden, Frida?" Vivian had noticed the plot of dirt I had started to dig up. Andreas examined the fruit bowl that Maggie kept on the counter. She knew that I liked kiwi fruit so she had bought a bag of them before leaving for Calgary.

Andreas seemed intrigued by the kiwi so I took one and cut it in half. I gave him one half with a small spoon and showed him how to scoop out the green flesh. He followed my lead and nodded in appreciation. "Thank you. It's wonderful." He was really into the kiwi, so I cut another one and told him to give the other half to Vivian. The two of them sat at the dining table. Vivian couldn't get the hang of scooping the flesh out so Andreas did it for her and fed her lovingly while she laughed. I watched them so a minute, but then I felt awkward and went to find Alex.

He was examining the pictures and books in the living room. Harold had a black and white photograph of workers on the Bloor Viaduct when it was first built. Harold always talked about that picture when people came to visit. "Look. No safety harnesses. No hard hats. Never get away with that now." Alex made no comment about the picture.

I asked him if he wanted a snack. "Andreas and Vivian are eating kiwi." Alex looked at me as if was trying to understand whether I was telling a joke. I led him to the hallway where we could see Andreas and Vivian sitting at the dining table, totally engrossed in one another and the kiwi.

Alex looked at me. "Do you have anything to drink?" I went upstairs and got the whiskey. I took out four glasses and we all drank.

Andreas and Vivian hated the taste of the whiskey. Vivian made a face after taking a sip. "My grandfather used to drink this." They went back to the bowl of kiwi.

Alex and I continued with the whiskey. He didn't comment on the whiskey, but I could sense him observing how I drank it without the kind of reaction that Vivian had. I considered for a minute whether I should pretend to find it too strong, but the first drink had already spread its warmth through me and I couldn't muster the play acting energy it would have required to grimace and struggle with each swallow. I just drank as I would have done on my own.

Alex kept pace with me and kept up a running commentary on the evils of suburban sprawl, car-centred neighbourhoods and mono culture lawns. It was getting dark and we didn't turn on any lights. Alex and I had moved into the living room. We sat on the couch which was big enough that we could sit a couple of feet apart with our bodies angled towards each other. The whiskey bottle sat on the coffee table in front of us. In the semi-darkness of the living room, I was watching Alex talk and drink when I realized that Andreas and Vivian had gotten quiet. The window of the dining room faced west so the last light of the day illuminated the table where they were sitting when I leaned over the back of the couch to look down the hall at them.

They had stopped eating kiwi and were kissing. Andreas leaned his long, thin torso across the corner of the table and Vivian supported herself with both hands on the chair seat beside her legs. I looked away immediately, but I felt desire rush through my body. Alex had not seen Andreas and Vivian. He continued to talk. Although he was used to monopolizing conversations, my absolute silence eventually caused him to slow down his monologue and then, to stop talking altogether. I leaned over to the coffee table to get more whiskey and managed to reposition myself closer to him. Our knees were almost touching and I inclined my upper body so that our heads were no more than a foot apart.

We both drank. Neither one of us spoke. I just looked at him. The whiskey had slowed me down and I felt I could sit there in silence looking at Alex forever. Miraculously, he did look back at me. He did smile. He did take our glasses and put them down on the coffee table. He did kiss me. He did move his hands over my body, first on top of my clothes, and then underneath them. He did lean into me and breathe heavily into my ear. "Can we go to your room?" And we did go to my room.

Afterwards it was dark. Alex got out of my small bed and went to the bathroom. I turned on my nightstand lamp and it lit up the room just enough to see the various pictures and other items I had around. Just like he had done downstairs, Alex started looking at these when he came out of the bathroom. "Is this your parents?" A picture of me with Harold and Maggie at Niagara Falls. I said that it was. Alex moved slowly around the room, looking at my things. In the half light his features were not clear but his presence filled the room. Items from my childhood were still on display. My stuffed letter "F", a framed character award from grade six for "Integrity". Seeing these items in the same room as Alex made me feel shy, but he didn't comment on those.

He focused on the framed picture from the allotment gardens. It had been taken not long after I started going there. Cecilia, Giuseppe and Carol were in the picture. Giuseppe looked serious, a little bit like those black and white pictures of farm workers you would see where the farmers are looking at the photographer as if to say "we've got work to do here. Why are you messing around with that camera?" Carol and Cecilia were laughing in the picture, laughing so hard it looks like they were holding each other up. This was typical of those two who could hardly communicate because Cecilia had almost no English, but they would play pranks on one another and just laugh uproariously all the time. Teresa and Lionel were there too, looking calm and capable. I was there too. I looked so young. My hair was messy and I had mismatched gardening gloves on. I was grinning. I remembered being just perfectly happy.

"Who are these people?" Alex picked up the framed picture and held it towards me.

"That was taken at the allotment gardens on Leslie Street. Those are people who had plots there."

This was interesting to Alex and he brought the picture back to the bed and asked me to explain about the allotment gardens and who all the people were. I was happy to do this except when it came time to explain who Lionel was, Alex could tell there was more to the story then I was telling.

"Did you date?" It wasn't a jealous question. I got the sense that Alex wanted me to have dated Lionel. I tried to explain how it was with him and Alex nodded and encouraged me and before I knew it I had told him all about the Labour Day weekend BBQ and Lionel being questioned by the cop.

"Holy shit! He just interrogated him there for no reason? Just for being with you?" Alex was incensed. Strangely, I thought, he was way angrier than Lionel had been that day. I remembered the look on Lionel's face when he told me that he had been questioned eight times by police just that summer. I didn't tell Alex this. I thought he might explode.

"So what happened? Did you have to go to hearings and all that?"

"What do you mean, hearings?"

"Like, disciplinary hearings for the cop."

"No. There was nothing like that."

Alex was quiet for a minute. "Frida. What happened when you filed a complaint against the cop?"

There was no way out. I had to tell the truth. "We never filed a complaint."

Alex was quiet again. "You didn't say anything to the cop at the time? Like ask him why he was harassing your friend?"

"No."

"And when it was clear afterwards that the cop had questioned your friend as an act of racist policing you didn't bother to go file a complaint?"

"No." I took the framed picture from Alex and hugged it to my chest.

Alex got out of the bed and searched around for his clothes. I had no way to justify what I hadn't done so I just watched him. "You know Frida," Alex stood by the bedroom door, "to defeat systemic racism people with privilege, like you," I felt he was stabbing me with his words, "Like. You." and I winced. "People with privilege like you need to stand up and speak out. If you stay quiet, you are complicit." With that, Alex left.

It was just after nine p.m. After I heard the door close behind Alex I went downstairs. Vivian and Andreas had left too. The house was empty. I checked my phone. Vivian had sent me a message:

thx 4 kiwi (heart emoji)
txt me later with details (sexy wink emoji).

I didn't text Vivian. I scrolled through my chats until I found Sandra. I knew she wasn't there. I had had no response to texts for weeks and one day I had tried to call and got the "this numer is out of service" message. I opened the chat anyway. I wrote the following message:

Met someone. His name is Alex. We had sex. He hates me.

I touched send even though I knew she wouldn't ever look at it. After looking at my phone blankly for a few minutes, I went to find the whiskey bottle.

I didn't go to school the next day. Harold and Maggie came home from Calgary and I told them that I had caught a flu bug. I stayed in my room for three days. Maggie would bring me soup and ask me if I wanted her to call the doctor.

Vivian messaged me a couple of times. You good? What happened with Alex? I just replied that I was okay and gave her the same flu bug story to explain why I wasn't in school. I figured I would have to go back eventually, but at that moment I just couldn't face Alex.

One of the things that I did while holed up in my room was to purge all the childlike things that had made me feel so awkward when Alex had looked at them. I couldn't bring myself to actually throw them away, but I gathered them all together to hide in the back of the closet. I looked at the allotment garden picture for a long time trying to decide what to do with it. Alex's rebuke had stung me and I felt he was right to blame me for being complicit. I was willing to own up to that as the person I was, sitting in my room at that moment, but I was not ready to blame the me that I saw in the picture. Even though the me that was in the picture was the person who had failed to act. Instead of blame, when I looked at that picture I felt compassion. I decided to keep the picture where it had been displayed on my bookshelf.

In the closet I found a box that I figured would be perfect for my stuffed letter "F", my grade six "Integrity" award and the other items I wanted rid of, or at least hidden from view. The box was a decent size, but it was very light. At first I thought it was empty and I wondered why Maggie would stash an empty box in the back of my closet. It wasn't empty. There was a manilla envelope in the bottom of the box with my name written on the front. In the top lefthand corner of the envelope was a stamp, not a postage stamp, but a printed stamp like what they would use to put the school name inside of textbooks. This stamp read "Children's Aid Society of Toronto" and there was a logo - an image of a small child sitting inside a letter C.

The envelope hadn't been opened and I remembered what it was. When the social worker had come to tell me that my bio-Mom had died she told me that they had found some papers and pictures that I might like to have. A few weeks later she dropped off this envelope when I was at school. Maggie hadn't opened it. When I got home from school she had showed me the envelope and asked whether I wanted to open it on my own. I remembered looking at the envelope and not wanting to see what was inside. The images and sensations that I associated with Arlene were all traumatic. Even though this would never have been the case, I imagined that the pictures in that envelope would be of Arlene lying dead under a bridge in Vancouver or shooting up in a crappy Downtown East Side apartment. I thought about opening it many times, but eventually I stopped thinking about it. I guess Maggie must have put it in the box in my closet.

Now was the right time to open the envelope, and that is what I did. There wasn't too much in there. There was the document about my adoption that the social worker had explained was what led the police to find me to notify me about Arlene's death. There was an Ontario driver's licence with a 2001 expiry date and an address on Ulster Street in Toronto. Arlene looked quite good in the picture, there was a plumpness about her face. There were four or five pictures of a bunch of people beside a lake. People were posed for pictures in camping chairs with cans of beer. They looked to be in their early twenties. Most of the guys were shirtless and they all had tattoos on their arms or their chests or both. The women in the pictures were all wearing shorts, tank tops and flip flops. At first I wondered if it was some kind of uniform, but there wasn't any logo on the shirts and there was enough variety in the styles (one tank top had slightly larger straps, some of the shorts were pattered, while others were solid colours) that I decided it was not a uniform, just an agreed upon outfit.

I looked at these pictures for a while before I spotted Arlene. She was in the background. The foreground was a well-muscled guy holding a can of beer up to the camera. His mouth was open and his face was animated, so I guessed that the photographer had caught him while he was giving a toast. Arlene was behind him and looking at him with a tolerant expression like she would let him finish what he was saying and then tell him to sit down. Beside Arlene, slightly blocked by the muscled toast maker, was a guy wearing a brown baseball cap. His face wasn't clearly visible, but that baseball cap was familiar. I was pretty sure it was my dad. He was in a chair next to Arlene and he would have been totally blocked by the guy giving the toast except that my dad was leaning towards Arlene like he was going to tell her something that was just for her to hear. His arm was resting on the armrest of her chair.

There was one picture with Arlene, my dad and me. I was a baby but not a newborn, because I was holding myself upright in Arlene's arms. She was looking at the camera proudly. It must have been summer because the picture was taken on a beach and Arlene was wearing a sleeveless top and her face looked a bit sunburned. My dad was looking at me, making a funny face, and I was reaching out a pudgy hand to touch him. I looked at that picture for a long time. Finally I turned it over and saw written on the back in rounded, girlish handwriting, "Me and

Luke with Frida at Sauble Beach." Luke. My dad's name was Luke. I didn't remember anyone telling me that, but it felt like something I had known.

I took the Sauble Beach picture and stood it beside the allotment garden one. I thought of Alex picking up the Sauble Beach picture and coming over to ask me about it. The thought of what his reaction would be to the story of that picture made me smile because I knew that I would never tell Alex that story.

UNIVERSITY
APPLICATION

———— ⅰ|ⅰ| ————

Maggie knocked gently on my bedroom door the following day. She poked her head in "Frida, dear? Feeling better?"

November had come to an end and this was a bright winter day like the ones you get in December after an early snowfall. The sun was relentlessly bright and it had propelled me out of bed almost against my will. Maggie was half surprised to see me out of bed. I gave her a hug. "Much better. Is there any food?"

Maggie's face, that had been twisted with worry since returning from Calgary, relaxed a little. "Yes! Of course there is food. What can I make you?" We went downstairs and Maggie made eggs and toast and I put the coffee on. I could tell by the way she was looking at me that she had something she wanted to say.

"What's up?"

Maggie put the eggs and toast on a plate and gave it to me together with a knife and fork. "The school called," she said with a forced cheerfulness.

"What for?" I bit into the toast.

"They want us to go in with you to talk to the guidance counsellor."

"Why?" I had an idea, but I thought it would be better to play my cards close to my chest.

"It seems that you haven't done your university application yet." Maggie had poured herself a coffee and was grasping the mug with a white-knuckle grip.

"Well, not yet. I've been sick."

"It seems that the last day to submit an application is right after the break and most students have already put theirs in." Maggie paused and took a sip of coffee. "Weeks ago."

"Okay. So when are we supposed to go meet this guidance counsellor?" I didn't want to dicuss my university application. I had absolutely no idea which university I wanted to go to, or even if I wanted to go to university, but I knew that was not even open for discussion. I had done no research into different universities or programs. Harold, Maggie and Paul had all gone to Queens, so I figured, worst case scenario, I would just apply there and they wouldn't question it.

Maggie didn't ask any more questions. I think she was just so happy that I had gotten out of bed and hadn't put up any objections to going to talk to the guidance counsellor.

The following day Harold, Maggie and I drove to school to meet the guidance counsellor. Harold talked most of the ride about Queens and how it had changed since he and Maggie had gone there. "When we went to take Paul we couldn't believe all the new buildings, eh, Maggie?" I remembered Paul leaving for Queens. I was only seven so I didn't really understand what was going on. I remembered feeling a vague sense of worry for Paul that he was going to be living away from home. If he did have any problems adjusting to University life, Harold and Maggie kept them from me. He was only home for a few weeks at a time over the next few years and when he was home, he had very little interest in me. He brought me a Queens scarf one year, that was about it.

Harold parked the car and we went in. I was relieved that it was class time so chances were good that I wouldn't see Alex. When we got to the guidance office the secretary told us to go through to an inside office and that Mr. Petroff would be with us in a minute. I had never met Mr. Petroff one on one although I had seen him give course selection and career planning presentations. I imagined that had no idea who I was. He probably ran some kind of report on grade twelve university applicants and my name came up with nothing. I could picture him looking at my name and student number on a list and scratching his head. "Frida? Who is that?"

When Mr. Petroff came into the office and saw me, he did have a glimmer of recognition. I had, after all, been a student here since grade nine, he must have at least seen me in the hallway. Mr. Petroff introduced himself to Harold and Maggie and we all sat down in his office. It was a little cramped. There was an extra chair and Maggie asked whether she could move it into the outer office to give us more space.

"Actually we're going to need that. One of Frida's teachers will be joining us any minute." Mr. Petroff was looking at his computer, pulling up my records and the university application site. My back was to the door of the office, so I couldn't see who it was, but I heard the guidance secretary speak.

"Nice to see you, Vladimir! They are waiting for you in Mr. Petroff's office."

I could hardly believe it when I heard a familiar voice reply. "Thank you, Donna. I am moving slowly. But I am getting here eventually." I turned around in my chair and, sure enough, Mr.

Vakarovsky was making his way towards us. I couldn't contain my joy. I jumped out of the chair and went towards him.

"Mr. Vakarovsky! Oh my God! I didn't know you would be here!" Before I knew it I was crying and Vakarovsky was patting my shoulder.

"Is okay, Frida. Maybe you thought I was dead? No. I am alive. Not a ghost, don't worry!"

This made everyone laugh and I managed to pull myself together and sit down. I was so happy. I just looked at Vakarovsky talking to Harold and Maggie and explaining about the gardening club. "But the doctors told me it was not the digging that brought the heart attack. They said I could have been sitting in a chair all day, same thing would have happened." Vakarovsky looked the same, maybe a little thinner, but his voice was strong and his eyes were clear and bright. I began to wonder if perhaps Mr. Petroff hadn't seen my name on a list of grade twelve applicants to university. Maybe Vakarovsky had asked about me and found out that I hadn't applied.

I wasn't really paying attention to what was being said, but I realized that everyone had stopped talking and was looking at me. "What do you think, Frida?" Maggie asked.

"Obviously it's good to follow your passion." Harold was talking equally to Mr. Petroff and Mr. Vakarovsky as he was to me. "If Frida is passionate about ... plants," he paused before saying "plants" as if to make sure he didn't say it with too much scorn, "horticulture is a perfectly reasonable program to apply to." Although this was a statement, Harold said it with a question in his voice.

"Maybe you are thinking is just for farmers," Vakarovsky never shied away from saying what others would only hint at, "but it is very good program. Highly respected."

"Frida should not put all her eggs in one basket. We would like her to apply to Queen's as well." Maggie laid her hand on Harold's arm to let him know that she knew what he was thinking.

Mr. Petroff showed me the University Application site and how to select the programs I wanted to apply for. "There are plenty of other options, Frida. You don't need to decide today." Petroff gestured towards the wall of his office where dozens of University brochures were displayed. The array of shiny booklets featuring pictures of impossibly confident people was too intimidating to even consider.

"No, I think I'm ready to go for those two." I was desperate to end this "planning Frida's future" session as quickly as possible.

Petroff smiled. "Okay, then. I will just print out the details of the schools and programs we have discussed here today. You have your Personal Identification Number for the application site and you know about the application fee." Here he looked at Harold and Maggie who nodded gravely. He handed me the papers and I looked at the Horticulture one. "University of Guelph" it said. I had never heard of that university and I wasn't exactly sure how to pronounce "Guelph".

"Where is this horticulture program, exactly?" I looked at Vakarovsky.

"Is not far from the city. Guelph is nice small town. You will like it. The rent will be cheaper than Toronto for student housing."

"Guelph." I practiced saying it while the adults stood up and started saying their goodbyes.

Mr. Petroff spoke to me, but with the clear goal of letting Harold and Maggie hear what was being said. "I know that you have been sick, Frida, but you'll have to get your marks back up before they get sent to the universities."

"Frida will come to do extra math work." Vakarovsky made no pretence of speaking to me, he addressed Harold and Maggie directly. "The last few weeks have been relaxing time. Now that I am back, the work will start."

Mr. Petroff looked a little nervous. "Of course we will not expect Frida to overdo it, since she has been ill. Just as much as she is able to do."

Vakarovsky waved his hand at this. "Yes, yes. Nobody will go to hospital. I have just come out of there. Food is terrible."

We went home and logged into my Ontario University Application account. Harold and Maggie stood behind me and handed over a credit card at the right moment. I put applications in to Queen's University and the University of Guelph. I practiced saying "Guelph" under my breath as I watched the swirling "processing" icon absorb my information.

The idea that I could be accepted to attend university and that I would leave Toronto to go there was a foggy concept that seemed as probable in that moment as winning the lottery or meeting a celebrity. I knew it had made Harold and Maggie happy and probably Vakarovsky too, so that was enough for me. At least when I went back to school on Monday I would have some place to go at lunch. I recognized the gleam in Vakarovsky's eye. There was a lot of math in store for me.

ESSAY WRITING

Mr. Petroff had told me that I needed to get my marks up, but I didn't understand how difficult that was going to be. I had never been particularly disciplined when it came to school work. I had always had decent marks, but not through any extraordinary effort on my part.

Math turned out to be the easiest to improve. With Vakarovsky coaching me I was able to get back on track quickly. Chemistry and biology were a little harder, but I discovered some good YouTube tutorials that I watched over and over again until the mysteries of covalent bonds and molecular genetics revealed themselves to me. English was the biggest problem. We were reading *In the Skin of a Lion* and I had no idea what it was about. We had an essay to write and I didn't know how I was going to get it done. The fact that Alex and Vivian were in my English class didn't help. I only attended the bare minimum of classes to avoid the teacher calling home. When I was there I tried to make myself as small as possible. Alex had made no attempt to contact me and I had ignored Vivian's texts since coming back to school. They sat together in class, but they didn't seem to talk to one another very much and Vivian would sometimes stay behind at the end of class telling Alex, "you go ahead. I'll catch up."

The essay was due in three days. I had stayed behind after class to talk to the teacher. Maybe I could get an extension or an alternative project to do. Vivian had stayed behind as well, and one other girl: Constantina. She was also struggling with her essay, but at least she had a first draft and wanted to go over it with the teacher. Constantina got to the teacher first and they sat at the desk at the front of the room going over the draft. Vivian and I sat awkwardly in our desks. I was looking at my phone. Vivian was reading a book, not the one for class. The discussion of Constantina's first draft was taking forever, but I knew I couldn't leave. I heard Vivian shuffling her stuff together, and I thought, "thank God. She's leaving." But instead of leaving, she came and stood beside my desk.

"Hey Frida." Vivian didn't look at me directly, she positioned herself so that her back was towards the teacher and she perched on a desk slightly in front of and to one side of where I was sitting. "Having a little trouble with your essay?" Because of her stutter it took a longer than normal time to ask this, but even so, the way she asked was not unkind, and I was grateful that she hadn't opened with the awkward "what happened with Alex?" question.

I rolled my eyes. "I haven't even started. I don't get this book at all."

Vivian smiled. "It's a little difficult for sure." She didn't seem stressed at all.

"How's your essay coming?"

Vivian shifted slightly on the desk so that she could look at me more directly. "I'm done." She said this matter-of-factly, not as a boast.

I sighed. "That must be a wonderful feeling."

The teacher was now trying to explain to Constantina the importance of using quotes from the novel in her essay. Vivian gave me an incredulous look. "If you like, I can help you with your essay."

I didn't hesitate. "Would you? Thank you so much!" I wished that I could offer to help her with one of her courses, but I knew she was taking history, social science and photography, so I had nothing.

We left the classroom and decided that we would go to my house to work on the essay. Vivian was amazing. She never mentioned Alex. I saw her go on her phone for a minute and I guessed that she was texting Alex or Andreas, but she didn't say anything about them. It was a cold day, so we buttoned up our coats, I put on my hat and Vivian wrapped a scarf around her head to keep her ears warm. She took my arm as we headed out into the wind and snow. "Ok, Frida! Let's go. By tonight you'll be Ondaatje's biggest fan! You'll see." I doubted that, but I was willing to try.

Over the next three days Vivian basically re-told me the whole book. She explained everything that had made no sense to me when I read it. Her copy had a different cover than the one I had from the school. She had bought her own copy and had filled it with sticky notes and comments. I had never seen anyone read a book like that. Vivian's stutter got less and less pronounced the more she talked about the book. Sometimes she would read a passage aloud to me and when she did that, she didn't stutter at all. I was floored. Somehow she got me to write the essay. I worried that the teacher would think that Vivian had written it for me because I felt like I never would have been able to write a thing if not for Vivian.

"Oh, don't worry." Vivian was not concerned. "My essay is totally different." She gave me her essay to read, and it was totally different from mine even though I felt like mine was a product of Vivian's brain. I could see that the teacher would never think that the same person had written the two essays. Mine was okay. When reading it you would think that I had read the book and had something to say about it. Vivian's essay was genius. It was easy to read, but not simplistic. It reminded me of how Vakarovsky would explain a complex math problem. He made the solution seem obvious, and if you followed his explanation closely it unfolded like a flower coming into bloom. Vivian's essay was like that. After reading it, I felt a little shy to talk to her. If Vivian noticed my shyness, she didn't comment on it. She proposed that we have a drink to celebrate. My bottle of whiskey was almost empty. I poured our drinks. Vivian asked if I had anything to mix the whiskey with since she found it too strong to drink on its own. I didn't know anything about mixing drinks, but I knew someone who did.

"Let's call Tomasz!" I was pleased to think of Vivian meeting Tomasz. I felt that they would like one another. I got him on video chat so they could see each other's faces.

"I was starting to think you were dead, Frida! Why haven't you called? Are you done with the flu now?" Tomasz would not admit it, but I could tell that he had been worried about me.

"Yes, Tomasz. I am much better. This is my friend Vivian! She just helped me do my English essay!" Vivian and Tomasz did a virtual 'nice to meet you' wave. "Tomasz, I need your advice on mixing drinks."

"Make it quick, Frida. I need to get ready for work in a minute." Tomasz told me to mix the whiskey with ginger ale and he told me to bring Vivian along to Calliope that weekend. He passed the phone to Shakil while he went to get ready for work.

Vivian mixed a tiny splash of the whiskey with ginger ale and I mixed a tiny splash of ginger ale with my whiskey and we toasted our success. Shakil admired Vivian's hair and said that, if she wanted, he would do her make up for going to Calliope.

Vivian laughed. "I don't really wear makeup, but I'll give it a try." Vivian, I could tell, was not like me. I loved to have Shakil do my clothes and makeup so that I could transform into Flower Power. Vivian saw it as a fun thing to try on, but her normal personality was already full and powerful and she didn't need makeup to gain confidence.

I guess I was staring at Vivian while these thoughts were going through my head because she was looking at me strangely and asked whether I was okay. Shakil piped up, "yeah, Frida, what's been going on with you? You've been all silent and sullen for a couple of weeks now."

Maybe the whiskey was starting to have its effect. Without thinking, I started to explain what had happened with Alex. Shakil and Vivian listened as I explained that we had gone up to my bedroom. I didn't go into details about the sex, but Shakil was happy to hear that we did have sex. He did a little dance and yelled to Tomasz in the bathroom. "Frida finally got laid!" I was a little embarrassed by the "finally", but I laughed when Tomasz stuck his head out of the bathroom with his toothbrush in his mouth to give me a thumbs up.

I didn't hold back anything. I told them about Lionel being questioned by the police in exactly the same way I had told Alex. I realized as I was doing this, that they might react in the same way that Alex had reacted and I might lose not only Vivian, but Tomasz and Shakil. I had gone too far in the telling, the words came out in an unbroken stream. When I finished telling how Alex had told me off and then left I felt emptied out and numb. I sat looking at my glass and waited to hear what they would say.

Shakil brought the phone right up to his face. "You mean to tell me that this guy…" Shakil held up one finger, "… comes to your house and drinks your booze …" Shakil held up a second finger, "… goes up to your bedroom and has sex with you,…" Shakil held up a third finger, "… starts interrogating you about your past boyfriends, ..." Shakil held up a fourth finger, "... gives you, all ninety-eight pounds of you, grief for not ending systemic racism by standing up to a fully-armed police officer at the side of the road!?" Here Shakil seemed to feel he had run out of fingers and just wagged his hand in exasperation. "Frida, you are better off without this guy, and I am sorry, Vivian, if he is your friend, but he sounds like an asshole."

Shakil's reaction gave me the courage to look at Vivian. She didn't say anything at first and I had a sinking sensation that she felt like Alex did, that I should have stood up to the cop. That I should have done something to speak up for Lionel. Vivian's facial expression was hard to read. She didn't seem mad, either at me, like Alex had been, or at Alex, like Shakil was. She just looked a little sad. The silence was about to be awkward, when she spoke to me. "I'm sorry that Alex treated you like that, Frida." She gave me a hug. "Believe me, it's not really about you. He's got his own problems."

Shakil softened his outrage after Vivian said that. "Well, we all have problems, that's for sure!" Tomasz had finished getting ready for work by this time and needed his phone back. We all said our goodbyes with promises to meet up that weekend at Calliope.

Vivian got a text from her mom saying that she was needed at home, so she left. I finished the whiskey bottle and tried to imagine what Alex's problems were. Looking at Alex, you would never imagine that he had problems. He was good-looking, tall and powerful, with nice clean clothes and clear skin. He aced all his classes. He seemed to know everything about everything. That night I dreamed that Alex was giving a presentation in English class. He was talking away confidently until the teacher interrupted him except that it wasn't our English teacher, it was Shakil. Shakil as English teacher starting questioning Alex and challenging him on his work, holding up one finger at a time to enumerate his errors. Alex took his seat without another word.

ALEX'S PROBLEMS

Alex approached me when I was at my locker after classes the following week. It was the final week of classes before the winter break. "Hi, Frida. Can I talk to you?" Alex was embarrassed. "Vivian said I should apologize to you about what I said the other night." I could see that he was suffering, and I remembered what Vivian said about him having problems of his own.

"It's okay Alex. I guess you have some strong feelings about things." I tried to speak lightly, but having him close to me was making it very difficult to be cool and calm. He grabbed the lock that was attached to the locker next to mine. He leaned away from the lockers while holding on to the lock, like a kind of anchor.

"I know I behaved like a dick to you. I'm a little messed up, you know?"

"I understand. And I guess I kind of deserved some of what you said to me."

"No, Frida." Alex let go of the lock and put his hand on my arm. "I need you to understand that none of that stuff that I said was really about you." He let go of my arm and grabbed onto the lock again. This time he leaned his forehead against the locker like he was trying to hide his face. I felt badly for him. Whatever it was that made him say those things to me was obviously eating at him. Maybe it would have been better to just tell him that I understood. That it was okay. Maybe it was the way he was standing with his head bowed like a guilty child, but I felt that he wanted me to demand an explanation.

"If it wasn't about me, Alex, you better tell me what it was really about."

Alex lifted his head and looked at me. "Yes." He looked up and down the hall. There were still plenty of students milling around. "Not here. Can we go to a coffee shop or something?"

"Sure. I know just the place."

*   *   *

Lieberman's was not busy, so Alex and I were able to get a booth to ourselves. I hadn't been at Lieberman's since the summer and I felt a pang when I passed the counter where I had sat with Sandra after the shooting. We ordered coffee and pastries. Alex fidgeted with his spoon, but he didn't eat or drink while he told me about Ballantyre School for Boys.

"Ballantyre is one of the top schools for rich families in Ontario. We're talking UCC is here ..." Alex put up his hand near his eyes to indicate a high level, "... and Ballantyre is right up there." He put his other hand beside the first one and moved his hands up and down slightly to indicate a more or less equal footing. I didn't like to ask what UCC was, so I just nodded and put on an impressed face.

"My Dad is head of global custody for TD and he will have nothing but the best for his boy." Alex used his "lord of the manor" voice to give this information. "I was a boarding student from the age of twelve. At first it was great. We would all goof around together, play sports and put on shows. There were no girls, so we all didn't care how we looked. I'm an only child, so for me it was wonderful to have so many people my own age around." I tried to picture Alex as a twelve-year-old boy running around with a bunch of private school kids. I didn't have much in the way of reference to conjure up this picture. In grade eight we had been on a field trip to the museum and there was a class there from a private school. This one was boys and girls, but they all had uniforms, like with actual blazers with a crest on the front. I remembered watching them with fascination.

Sandra had whispered to me. "Why are all those kids white? Is it some kind of Nazi school?" I had shrugged. I noticed the whiteness, but also the girls' hair was all perfectly smooth and the boys lacked the excessive video-gaming pallor that white boys at Thornton Middle School had. They were clear-eyed and alert. They may as well have been aliens.

"Did you have a uniform with a blazer?"

Alex looked at me blankly. "Yeah. It was navy blue."

"Oh. Sorry to interrupt. Keep going." I drank some of my coffee and took a bite of the cherry danish.

Alex continued. "Around grade nine things started to change. Almost all the students were from rich families, but some were, like, super-rich, and others were just, like, both parents are surgeons rich. And a few were there on scholarships. They had gone through some intense application process and were math geniuses or played the violin or something."

The regular waitress with the teased blonde hair came to check on us. She saw that Alex hadn't touched his coffee or danish. "What's the matter, honey? You too nervous to eat?" She looked at me. "Why's he so nervous? I can see that he's a fine eater normally." She stood back and observed with approval how Alex filled his side of the booth.

Alex blushed and looked happily at the waitress. He seemed pleased. "I'm going to eat it now. It looks delicious. I'm just telling a long story."

The waitress nodded and put her finger to her lips to stop herself from talking.

"Like I was saying, some of the boys were from super rich families and had started to kind of separate themselves from the rest of us. A couple were shy about it and would downplay the private jet holidays and luxury car birthday gifts, but then there was a group who were complete assholes. They made sure everyone knew they were the top of the hierarchy. They even called themselves Masters of the Universe." Alex's jaw tightened and he finally took a sip of his coffee.

"At the beginning of grade ten two new kids came to the school. One was on a full academic scholarship. His name was Jacob. His parents were organic farmers and he had been home-schooled until grade nine. He told us that when he went to his local high school he was way more advanced than any of the other students. He had read everything. He blew through math and science and French and geography. He didn't know how to keep a low profile. He would correct the teachers and get impatient with the other students 'because they were imbeciles'. Obviously he made himself very unpopular.

"By Christmas he was miserable and the school recommended he apply for a scholarship to Ballantyre. They told his parents to enrol him in some camps or something so he could learn how to get along with other kids. By the time Jacob came to Ballantyre he was a little better. He figured out not to correct the teachers in front of the class and just brought a book to read when he had finished his work and everyone else was struggling to get through. He tried, but it must have felt like everyone else was operating on half speed and he was impatient. He was strong too, from working on his parents' farm. If he had been from a rich family he could have been the star of the school, but because he was a poor kid from the country who didn't know how to be quiet, the "masters of the universe" decided that he needed to be slapped down.

"Jacob was strong, but he wasn't that good at team sports having never played on any teams before. He was naturally athletic and listened carefully to the coaches instructions, but he just didn't have the experience with the rules and techniques. Ballantyre's most important team was the rugby team. Jacob tried out and made the team, but he wasn't a star player.

"The other new student that year was a kid named Marcus. His mother worked in the school office. He was one of only two black kids at the school. The other was the son of a Nigerian businessman. He had been at the school as long as I had. Marcus had earned a scholarship like Jacob had, and his mother's position as employee entitled them to a further discount, so that's how he came in. He was smart, but he knew how to get along with other kids so he found a friend group with the son of a dentist and a musical prodigy and he didn't cause waves. He wasn't exactly friends with Jacob, but because they had started together and they were both outsiders, they were kind of allied."

Alex took another sip of coffee. I could see he was reluctant to tell the next part of the story. A few more people had come in since we had sat down, and the sounds of plates and cups rattling and people talking was a little louder. I sat quietly and waited for him to continue. "I wasn't one of the Masters of the Universe, obviously, but they saw me as a reliable underling. So one of them came to me before rugby practice and said 'We're going to need you to act as look out today. We're going to teach Jacob a lesson.'

"I didn't know exactly what he meant by 'teaching Jacob a lesson' but I knew it wasn't going to be pleasant for Jacob. I don't know why I went along. He was so light-hearted when he told me, it would have been weird to refuse. It would have been like you asking me to go to Lieberman's and me going 'No! I won't go along!'" I had a really bad feeling about what was going to happen to Jacob.

Alex continued. "After the rugby practice the Masters of the Universe cornered Jacob in the change room. The rest of the team left as if nothing was going on and I got the signal to keep watch by the change room door. I was standing in the hallway. I felt a little anxious that we were going to get caught and ..." Here Alex paused and took the coffee spoon and stood it up like a sentinel on the table. "I guess I also felt a little proud that the Masters of the Universe had chosen me to be lookout." He laid the spoon down with disgust.

"I could hear noises from inside the change room. At first it was just low laughter and shuffling, then I heard, 'Hold him! Hold him! He's a strong bastard!' I started to get nervous about what was going on, but I just stood there like a fool."

"Oh my God, Alex! What were they doing to him in there?"

Alex didn't look at me. He continued. "So I was standing there listening to these noises coming from the change room and who should come down the hall but Marcus. He wasn't on the rugby team and he didn't know anything about the 'let's teach Jacob a lesson' plan. I think it was just pure chance that he came down the hallway right then. He saw me and was about to walk right by when he heard the noises coming from the change room. Marcus looked at me and I guess my face gave it away." Here Alex paused and looked at me. "Frida, do you know that Marcus didn't hesitate? He knew something bad was going on and he knew he might be putting himself in danger by intervening, but he didn't hesitate. He pushed me out of the way and went into the change room. I could hear him. 'What the hell do you think you are doing? Leave him alone!' I couldn't move. I was so ashamed. I just stood there while

Marcus saved Jacob. The Masters of the Universe came out of the change room laughing and jostling one another like the whole thing had been a joke. I waited a few more minutes until Jacob and Marcus came out. Jacob was white in the face and was walking slowly. Marcus had his arm around his shoulder and was talking in his ear. 'Don't worry about those assholes. They're just jealous.'"

Alex sat looking at his coffee cup. I could see that he felt ashamed of himself, that he felt so small for his role in the whole thing. But it was only because he had told me about Jacob and Marcus and the Masters of the Universe that I knew how he felt. Aside from a slight wilting in his posture anyone else looking at him would not know that he was carrying all that around with him. This inside knowledge of Alex made me feel so close to him. I wanted to come over to his side of the booth and put my arms around him. I might have done just that except that the waitress passed by at that moment and Alex called to her. "Hello?! Could I get a little more coffee please?" His voice was confident. He had straightened his shoulders and the pained expression had cleared. I stayed on my side of the booth.

I remembered that Alex had told me about this incident not because he needed comfort from me, but because Vivian had told him off for treating me badly. He needed to explain why he had behaved the way that he had. Having given that explanation he was back to his normal self. I wondered if, in future, he would react again the same way as he had with me or whether he would be more understanding.

"Is this Fair Trade coffee, do you think? Did you notice a sign on the door on the way in?" Alex craned his neck to look towards the door.

"What's Fair Trade coffee?" I knew I was opening myself up for a long lecture with this question, but I didn't mind. Alex launched into an explanation of coffee production, international trade, Columbian rebels and roasting techniques and I gazed at him and nodded with agreement. He could be as all-knowing as he liked, I had seen him standing, ashamed, in front of that change room door.

*   *   *

One night in mid-February, Shakil, Vivian and I went to Calliope. Tomasz had to work so he couldn't come along. It was bitterly cold but we weren't wearing coats since once inside Calliope it was always hot and we didn't want the bother of coats. Usually it was just a quick hop out of an Uber and the bouncer would wave us in, but something was off that night because as we pulled up in front of the club there were tons of people milling around on the sidewalk.

"What is this? National go to a gay dance club day? Why are there so many people?" Shakil was irritated. He asked the driver to wait for a minute and he rolled down the window to call out to someone from the crowd on the sidewalk. "Yoo hoo! What's going on? Are you all lining up to go in?"

A tall blonde guy in a tight white shirt leaned over to look into the car. His breath froze in the air as he spoke. "No. We were all inside when they turned off the music and said we had to leave. Something about burst water pipes."

"Oh shit. Okay thanks." Shakil rolled up the window.

"Now what?" Vivian had a difficult time getting permission to go out at night. Her mother relied on her a lot to help out with her younger brother. He was autistic and sometimes he was just too much for Vivian's mom to handle. Her Dad worked most nights as a waiter in a downtown hotel, but he had managed to get a night off so that he could stay home and Vivian could go out. Vivian didn't want her precious night out to be over so soon, and Shakil and I both understood that. Shakil didn't want to go to another club where we would have to line up to get in. Vivian and I didn't relish the idea of lining up in the freezing cold in our tiny skirts and heels.

It didn't take long for Shakil to think up a solution. "Let's go to Tomasz's work. He can get us cheap drinks!" Tomasz still worked at the cafe in the Eaton Centre for lunch, but he had picked up a bar-tending gig at a neighbourhood bar on Roncesvalles. They hired him because he could speak Polish to the old guys who would come in, but he looked young and hip for the crowd who would come out for drinks on the weekend. Tomasz told us that the bar had been there for more than twenty years and that it was a bit run down, but the drinks were cheap and the vibe was good. People would cram together at mis-matched table, drink beer and vodka and eat perogies and salted nuts.

Shakil texted Tomasz to give him a heads up and he messaged back that he would save us a table near the bar. When we got there we could see that, aside from five or six old Polish men who sat at the bar, everyone else was young. Mostly they sat in groups of four or six people. There was music playing, but not too loudly. People were talking and eating, drinking and laughing. I looked at Vivian to see if she was disappointed in the change from Calliope. She looked around and smiled. "I think we are a little over dressed." Of course she was right, we were dressed for a night of clubbing and fully made up while most of the other patrons wore what looked like vintage jackets or sweaters and the girls wore little or no make up.

We told Shakil that we would join him in a minute and we went to the bathroom to tone down our make up a little. The bathroom was a tiny one-stall deal, but Vivian and I squeezed in together giggling and wiping off the exaggerated eyes and lips Shakil had done for us. When we came out we saw that Shakil had someone sitting at the table with him. "This is Shanice. She works with me at The Bay."

"Nice to meet you! I love your blouse! You both look so glamorous!" Shanice was an energetic talker with an amazing, open laugh that made people sitting nearby smile just to hear it. Shanice had come to the bar with her cousin, but the cousin wanted to get home early and Shanice wanted to stay out, so when she saw Shakil, she said goodbye to the cousin and joined our group. We ordered food and vodka and within twenty minutes Vivian and I felt like we had known Shanice our whole lives.

"Oh yes. I'm from the suburbs too. Scarborough born and raised." Shanice told us that she had moved downtown with her cousin. They were both at Ryerson. "Are you girls eternally single like me? Let me tell you, we do our best to focus on our studies," here Shanice put on an angelic face and sat up straight and proper, "but there are just so many fine men that are awfully distracting! Believe me! I used to go and study in this one spot that overlooked the athletic field. Except that whenever I was there trying to study, the soccer team would be there practicing or track and field or I don't know what blessed sport they were playing, I just know that there were so many fit men running and jumping and taking they shirts off, I could get no work done!" Shanice fanned herself with a napkin to cool off from the recollection. "Now, I ask you, how can a girl settle down with just one man when there is an entire team to try out?"

Shakil laughed. "Shanice, don't lead these innocent lambs astray! They are just starting out in the dating game."

"Oh that's okay. We are all a little shy to start out. I used to think that no man would look at me because I am a little heavy, but I found out that there are plenty of men who like any kind of woman. And I also found out that I don't need to settle for just any man who looks my way." Shanice tossed her hair proudly. I loved listening to her and watching her emphasize her words with her hands and eyes.

"I was lucky." Vivian brought up a picture of Andreas on her phone. The picture had been taken at school. Andreas would always wait by her locker for Vivian to come out of class. In the picture he was leaning his back and one foot against the lockers. He had his head back and his eyes closed like he was trying to grab a quick nap standing up. The light and angle of the shot made lanky, awkward Andreas look beautiful.

Shanice looked at the picture and at Vivian and she nodded. "Yes. Looks like you were lucky."

"Don't ask about Frida's love life it's just too painful to hear that story again." Shakil ordered us another round of drinks and patted my hand kindly.

Shanice got a text and told us that some friends were having a house party nearby. "Let's go! Maybe Viv here has found true love, but me and Frida are still on the hunt!' Shanice lifted her glass to cheers with mine.

"You girls go ahead and have fun. I'll hang out here and go home with Tomasz. Shanice will take care of you." Shakil hugged us all, we waved goodbye to Tomasz and hopped into an Uber with Shanice. The vodka made me feel warm and relaxed. Shanice kept up a constant flow of words the entire ride and soon enough we had arrived.

The party was in an apartment that was part of an old house. Shanice told us that several students lived there. Music was playing, but not dance music. Most people were just talking. A group in the living room were smoking a joint. Shanice found her friend Monica in the kitchen. "Hey, Babe! This here is Frida and this is Vivian. I just met them, but they are so sweet and if possible we have to fix Frida up with someone because she has had a tragic love affair and needs to learn to love again." I was embarrassed and hoped nobody else had heard.

Monica rolled her eyes lovingly at her friend. "Oh my God, Shanice, you are the worst! You can't introduce someone like that!"

"Why not? What do you want, her academic credentials?" Shanice opened the fridge and took out three bottles for herself, me and Vivian.

"Don't listen to this crazy woman. I'm Monica, this is my place."

Shanice got me and Vivian settled into a corner of the kitchen and then went to the living room with Monica. Vivian was calm and composed as always. She put the bottle that Shanice had given her back into the fridge, washed out a glass and got herself some water from the tap. She offered me some, but I felt like the alcohol was helping me to relax in this strange situation and I didn't know how I would do if I started to sober up.

There were a bunch of flyers and notices struck to the fridge and to a cork board on the kitchen wall. Vivian went over to look at them. I sat drinking from the bottle that Shanice had given me, it was sweet and went down easily. Three people came into the kitchen, one guy and two girls, one blonde and one with wild curly hair. I recognized them as the group who had been smoking up in the living room when we came in. I felt awkward sitting by myself so I stood up and smiled at them. The vodka from the Roncesvalles bar together with the sweet drink Shanice had given me hit all at once when I stood up. I felt wobbly and loose and I lost my balance a little. This struck me as hilarious so I started laughing hysterically. The three pot smokers also started laughing and we all kind of leaned into each other wobbling and laughing.

Finally the blonde girl caught her breath and looked at me. "Wait..." she tried to get serious and focus on my face. "Do we know you?" This was obviously hilarious and set us all laughing into each other's arms again. Out of the corner of my eye, I could see Vivian standing by the fridge with a bemused expression on her face.

"No really..." the guy stoner now tried to be serious. "What is your name?"

After another peal of laughter, I managed to speak. "Frida. My name is Frida."

"Oooh! Frida Kahlo!" the curly-haired girl said, "I love Frida Kahlo!"

This wasn't the first time I had someone bring up the Mexican painter when they heard my name, but I had never really gone to the trouble to find out much about her. When I was younger, the image of her with the famous unibrow made me a little embarrassed. I worried that I might develop a unibrow too because I had the name. Now the gushing reaction of the curly-haired girl made me feel proud of the association. "Oh yes! She's great!"

The blond stoner girl didn't know who Frida Kahlo was so the curly-haired girl started to explain. The stoner guy turned to me. He was slightly unsteady in his gaze and his words came out a little slowly but I could see that he was making an effort to appear less stoned than he really was. So I steadied myself by leaning a little against the kitchen table to try and appear less drunk than I really was.

"So you must go to OCAD." He leaned in close, and, although he smelled of weed, it was not unpleasant to have him come close to me. He had a short, neat haircut and an untroubled face. Even though he was a little unsteady just then, I could tell he was quite athletic. He had broad shoulders and a trim stomach. He steadied himself by leaning on the back of the kitchen chair. I noticed that his hands were sinewy with long, beautiful fingers. "Right? OCAD?"

I didn't have the wherewithal to pretend. "What's OCAD?"

He laughed. I laughed. He eventually realized that I didn't actually know what OCAD was. "You know. The art school." He had made the leap from my name to Frida Kahlo to art school in the type of logical connections that seem like flashes of genius to people in his state.

"No. I'm not an artist. I just have the same name as an artist."

"Got it. I'm Colin." Colin was not put off by the misunderstanding. Now, in order to avoid telling him that I was still in high school, I turned the conversation to him.

"What about you? Do you go to Ryerson?"

"Yeah. I'm in engineering." He said it like he was a little embarrassed. "I'm not like what you think an engineering student is." Colin was anxious that I understood he was not an average engineering student. He let go of the back of the kitchen chair and put his hand on my arm to emphasize his point.

Harold told some stories about being an engineering student at Queens but as far as I could remember they were all about first year students dying themselves purple. I didn't know if this was a Ryerson Engineering thing too, but he certainly didn't seem like the "dye yourself purple" type.

Colin left his hand on my arm and our eyes met. "You get it, don't you Frida?" He reached up and took a strand of my hair that had fallen across my cheek and tucked it behind my ear. "I'm not like those jerks."

I looked at him. I was still drunk of course, but when he had touched my arm and hair I felt a surge of energy that cleared my head a little. It wasn't unpleasant to have Colin touch my arm or even my hair. He was totally focused on me. The two other girls had moved towards the fridge and were talking with Vivian. He seemed to have forgotten about them and was adamant that I understand. "I am not like those jerks."

I smiled. "I can see that."

He smiled too and made a slight quivering movement like a mild electrical current had just run through him. "I feel like you do see me, Frida. Are you sure you are not an art student? You seem like you could be an art student."

I laughed. "No, I'm not an art student." He waited. I had to think of something to say that wouldn't give away that I was still in high school.

"I'm actually into horticulture."

He was intrigued. "Horticulture? Really? Like farming?"

"Yeah. There's a big future in urban farming you know. You engineers had better be on top of that." I tried to keep it light. I didn't want to have to go into too much detail because, although I knew a lot about plants and gardening, I couldn't fake being an actual horticulture student.

"Well, yeah! Everyone is growing their own weed!" The mention of weed made him remember his two stoner friends. He looked across the kitchen at them. I turned my head to do the same. I saw Vivian listening to the curly-haired girl. I hoped she was having a good time. Just as Colin and I turned to look at Vivian and the girls, two other people walked into the kitchen. The first was an incredibly beautiful girl. She was tall with dark skin and wonderful braided hair. She was wearing a little bit of makeup, a sprinkling of freckles and some iridescent eyeshadow, but I knew when looking at her that she would be just as beautiful, probably even more so, without the makeup. She was wearing thigh high boots and a maroon velvet skirt with a faded jean jacket. It was hard to know where to look, every part of her was so perfect.

Everyone in the kitchen stopped talking to gaze at this girl as she walked in. Right behind her came a guy dressed all in black. I must have been a little dazed by the girl because it took me a minute to register that I knew him. He saw me as soon as he came into the kitchen. A smile flooded his face as he recognized me. "Frida?"

I could hardly breathe. "Hi Lionel."

In March I turned nineteen. Harold and Maggie opened a bottle of champagne with my birthday cake and warned me not to drink too much. "There's a lot of drinking on University campuses Frida. You've got to be careful." Maggie didn't get into any specifics about I needed to be careful of. I assured her that I would be careful and I drank one glass of champagne. I fervently hoped that she was not going to try and give me advice about sex. Her explanation of the basic workings of the human reproductive systems had been mercifully quick and clinical. We had an Illustrated Guide to the Human Body that she directed me to if I had any further questions.

It wasn't the physical workings of the sex act that were puzzling to me. It was the emotional part, or the part that came before and after the sex act. How did you know if you wanted to have sex with someone and if they wanted to have sex with you? I understood, on the night of the Ryerson students' party that this was not always clear cut.

When Lionel walked in I felt an overwhelming attraction to him. His smile when he saw me made me think that he was also attracted to me. We had gotten to know one another well working together at the allotment garden and we always got along great. So I felt euphoric when Lionel hugged me and was genuinely happy to see me in the kitchen that night. But then he turned to the beautiful girl who had walked into the kitchen before him and introduced us. "Solange, this is Frida. She used to work with us at the allotment garden." Solange turned her beautiful gaze onto me for a brief glance. She took me in and discounted me in the space of four seconds. "Frida. This is my girlfriend Solange."

Somehow I managed to say something like "nice to meet you". Mercifully, Vivian must have seen my acute suffering and called to me. Went I went over to her, Vivian wrapped her arm around the small of my back and leaned over to speak quietly into my ear. "Oh my God. Is that Lionel?" I nodded wordlessly.

I was trying desperately not to cry. How could I have thought that he was interested in me? It was so obvious now when I looked at him with Solange that the way he felt about me and the way he felt about Solange were not in the same family of feelings. Vivian squeezed my waist. "Chin up, Frida. Don't let him see you cry."

At that moment I remembered Alex. I remembered how he looked so confident but was carrying around his shame that no one knew about. I realized that no one but Vivian would necessarily know that I was totally destroyed by seeing Lionel with Solange. If I could pretend that it didn't bother me, no one would know that it bothered me. I needed to act. I had never taken drama classes and I regretted it at that moment, but I did my best.

I joined in with Vivian and the two stoner girls and tried to avoid looking at Lionel and Solange, but I couldn't help watching them. They went to the fridge and took out some drinks. Lionel struck up a conversation with Colin and Solange took out her phone. I could see that although Colin was talking to Lionel, he kept looking at Solange. In fact, we all kept looking at her, it was impossible not to. She wasn't looking at anyone. She was looking at her phone and when she did eventually look up it was to gesture to Lionel with a movement of her head towards the door. "They're there." This was obviously the cue to leave. He took a swig from his drink and placed the two thirds full bottle on the table. Solange hadn't even opened hers, but he took that one and put it on the table too.

"We gotta bounce," he told Colin. "Nice talking to you."

Colin raised his drink to Lionel. "Yeah. Same." He didn't even bother trying to talk to Solange. Lionel stopped to say goodbye to me on the way out. "Frida, we are meeting some people at Secret City, so we gotta go now." He still smiled at me, but I kept my guard up. "It was so nice to see you again! Maybe we'll catch you at the gardens in the spring?" Solange moved impatiently. Lionel glanced at her. "Solange gets bored when I talk about the gardens." He said this like her getting bored was a admirable quality.

Solange ignored his comment and brought the conversation to a close by reaching out to shake my hand. "Yeah, nice to meet you. Enjoy your evening." Her hand was slim and cool and she offered it to me without energy. It was just a statement that she was done with me and I was dismissed. I had nothing to say. I just accepted the cool, slim hand, shook it gently and mumbled, "Yeah, you too."

After they left I felt a pit open in my stomach together with a sensation that I was covered with a really heavy blanket, so heavy, that I felt it would be hard to move. Colin got me a drink and I drank it quickly. Vivian went to the living room with the blonde and the curly-haired. The music was getting louder and I was having trouble hearing what Colin was saying.

"Let's go somewhere quieter." He had to lean in and say this in my ear and the sensation of his face brushing against mine gave me goosebumps.

He led me into a bedroom at the end of the hall. There was a dresser littered with makeup, hair brushes and hair products. A few people had put their jackets and bags on the bed. Colin piled these up on one end of the bed and we sat on the bed together. Even though we didn't turn the lights on in the room it was not completely dark. Light from the streetlights came through the uncurtained window and we hadn't closed the door all the way, so some light came in from the hallway.

Colin was quiet and I couldn't see his face very clearly. We were sitting side by side on the bed. "Could I kiss you, Frida?" Colin brushed his hand over my arm. A part of me was still trying to act like I wasn't destroyed by seeing Lionel and Solange, another part of me was enjoying the attention and closeness of Colin's body. All of me was very drunk. I shifted myself on the bed so that I had one leg bent underneath me and my body was turned towards him. Although he had asked to kiss me, he didn't make any move to do it. I didn't want to close my eyes because I was afraid the room would start spinning. I leaned towards Colin and kissed his mouth. He kissed me back, but he didn't touch me with his hands. I stopped kissing him and moved my head back a little to look at him. He was looking at me, but he didn't say or do anything. I remembered with Alex that as soon as we started kissing he had a hungry energy in his touch that led, without question, to sex. Here with Colin I couldn't tell if he wanted to have sex with me. He was still and calm and this made me unsure.

Vivian appeared at the door. "Here you are!" She looked back and forth from me to Colin. "You about ready to go, Frida?"

Colin didn't say anything.

I unfolded my leg from underneath me and got up off the bed unsteadily. "I guess so."

Colin took a hold of my hand. "Can I get your number?"

Vivian took a step inside the bedroom. "Why don't you give her yours?" The three of us were silent for a few seconds. Some had put Kaytranada on in the other room and the hypnotic beat floated into the bedroom. "Here, Frida. Give me your phone." Vivian took my phone and opened "add contact" then she passed it to Colin.

He entered his number and handed the phone back to me. "Text me whenever."

Vivian guided me out of the apartment and into an Uber. As we rode home I lay my head on Vivian's shoulder.

"Did you make out with that guy?"

"Kind of."

"Are you going to text him?'

I looked out the window of the Uber. We were stopped at a traffic light and a couple were crossing the road in front of us. The guy was tall with short reddish-blonde hair. He was wearing an army jacket. I couldn't be sure, but it looked a lot like Brian. The girl was shorter. She was further away from the car, so I couldn't see her as clearly. Just as they were almost across the street she stopped and reached back to fix her shoe which had slipped off the back of her foot. There was something very familiar about her. I sat up a little straighter in the seat to get a better look, but the light changed and our Uber pulled away.

Vivian poked me. "Frida!? What about it? Are you going to text him?"

I leaned my head back on her shoulder. "I don't know. Maybe."

WEDDING
ANNIVERSARY

———————— ı|ı ————————

Harold and Maggie had their thirtieth wedding anniversary that April. They had planned a party. Paul was coming from Calgary. Frank and Eileen were coming from the States. Other invitees were friends from work and neighbours. Paul arrived a few days before the party. He had put on a little weight and his hair had started to thin. He was looking more and more like Harold. The two of them spent long hours discussing the various projects Paul was working on. Two days before the party, they were having one of these sessions. Maggie could only stand about twenty minutes of engineering talk and then she would try to change the subject. "Are there any nice women that work with you, Paul? Have you gotten to know any nice places in Calgary?" Maggie had contacted a caterer to make food for the anniversary party and she had a plate full of samples of the finger food they were going to serve. She wanted us all to try them so we could finalize the order for the party.

Paul took a couple of mini quiches. "You know I'm working most of the time, Mom. I don't have too much time for getting to know Calgary." He avoided the question about women.

"I see." Maggie was disappointed, but she didn't push it. "What do you think about the quiches?"

Paul put one in his mouth, chewed thoughtfully and nodded. "Yep. Good."

"Okay. Well, you boys probably have a lot to talk about, so Frida and I will just finish selecting the food." Maggie looked like she might make a move to hug Paul, but then she hesitated and took the plate of samples out to the kitchen. She put the plate down on the counter with a sigh. "They are not much help, are they Frida? Thank God I have you." She hugged me and I felt like it was more than just for helping select mini quiches.

I hugged her back. "I'm lucky to have you too."

Maggie smiled. "Let's get to it. Shall we?" She laid out the catering menu on the counter and we spent the next hour finalizing the menu and discussing logistics for the party. What if it rains? Should we ask people to take off their shoes? As we talked, we could hear Paul and Harold in the other room. Their voices would rise and fall and sometimes they would laugh.

Maggie's friend Belinda, who she had known since she was a girl, was also coming to the party. She had moved to Vancouver before I came to live with Harold and Maggie, so I had never met her, but I felt as though I knew her because Maggie would talk about her quite often and she had a framed picture of the two of them as teenagers wearing short skirts and heavy eyeliner posing like models for a picture near some rocks beside a lake.

The day before the anniversary party, Maggie and I were looking at that picture together. "That's Ontario Place. Belinda and I used to go there in the summer." Maggie always got a happy expression looking at that picture. I liked looking at it too. Maggie looked so energized and free. "Belinda was the first person I met who had been adopted." Maggie explained. "When she started school this was a fascinating piece of information that got whispered around about her. I knew what being adopted meant, but I really wanted to know more about Belinda and her family. It wasn't hard because she lived on our street, just a few houses away. When my mother said that it was okay to go and play at her house, I went, full of curiosity about this adopted girl and her family."

Maggie got a far-away look when she talked about her childhood. Not dreamy, exactly, more like she was trying to recall and make sense of her memories and that it wasn't always an easy thing to do. When she told me about going to Belinda's house I got the feeling that this was a memory that she had recalled many times and had made sense of.

Maggie held the framed picture of her and Belinda as she explained her first impressions of the house. "It was a very clean house. Of course, ours was clean too, but this house was also sort of streamlined, new and shiny, whereas our was more worn and bare bones. I remember the carpet especially. It was soft and thick, a light grey that must have been extremely difficult to keep clean, although I didn't think of that at the time. Belinda's mother was a beautiful, well-dressed woman who was so pleased that Belinda had brought home a friend. She made snacks for us and was so pleasant, I was amazed."

Here Maggie looked at me. "I had trouble understanding why she was so nice to Belinda who wasn't even her own biological child. My own mother was never cruel, but she was not a kind, pleasant woman. I always was made to understand that I was an expense and a bother and I should do my best to be able to fend for myself as soon as possible." Maggie told me this without bitterness.

"Belinda's mother never said anything to her about how much it cost to feed and house her. She bought her nice clothes and, this was probably the most astounding thing, she would buy nail polish and the two of them would do each other's nails. This was a fantasy land in my eyes and I think it was then that I first got the idea that I would like to adopt a girl too one day. And I hoped to be like Belinda's mom." Maggie looked at me with a smile.

I wondered whether Maggie wanted me to say that she was just like Belinda's mom, but I felt awkward hearing her tell that story and imagining her trying to be like some fantasy world mom. To me Maggie just was and I didn't know the right thing to say or do. Maggie must have sensed my discomfort because she got up briskly and went to make tea. "All that was a long time ago, Frida. I can't believe that Belinda will be here tomorrow."

Belinda was one of the first to arrive on the day of the party. It was a bright, cold spring day. The snow had all melted, but the leaves had not come out on the trees yet so the light had an edge to it that highlighted the bare branches and winter damaged lawns.

Belinda was wearing a light spring coat and sandals. Maggie offered to take her coat when she arrived. "I think I'll keep it on for a minute. I forgot how cold Ontario is in April. We have flowers fully out in Vancouver already."

The two of them were so happy to see one another, they hugged for a full minute and laughed and cried. Maggie took her arm and they sat together in the living room talking hard like they were worried time would run out for them to say all they had to say.

I was to be a waitress and offer around the trays of food when people came. Paul was responsible for drinks. Even as more guests arrived it seemed that Maggie and Belinda were inseparable. They would talk to other people but they would gravitate back to each other and hold hands or put their arms around each other's waists. Harold had set up a photo station where people were supposed to pose with various funny hats and props from the eighties when they were married. Maggie and Belinda must have taken twenty photos there. As I watched them all I thought about was Sandra. Would I see her again? Would we be laughing and hanging on to each other in thirty years?

Most of the guests were gone by ten o'clock. The caterers were going to come to pick up the trays and rented glasses, plates and cutlery. Harold and Maggie were tired out but happy and sat in the living room talking. Paul and I were in the kitchen putting away the leftovers.

"So Harold tells me you are thinking of going to Guelph for horticulture." Paul said horticulture slowly like it was a word he had recently learned.

"Maybe I will. I haven't been accepted into the program yet." I stretched some plastic wrap over a plate of leftover quiches.

"So, you're into ... plants?" Paul was examining the remains of the anniversary cake. The guests had eaten almost three quarters of the large slab, but the remaining section was not a regular shape. The final row of pieces that had been sliced had not all been taken and the half row made a ragged edge to the remains of the cake with "ry" and "ie" from the "Happy Anniversary Harold and Maggie" that had been written on it in yellow icing.

I could see that this irregularity was troubling Paul so I cut off the uneaten remainder of the row, leaving a satisfying rectangle of leftover cake to go in the fridge. The offending partial row of cake I divided in half, giving one slice to Paul and one to myself. Paul nodded approvingly and took a fork full of cake which he held up to me. I also took a fork full of cake and held it up to him. "To ... horticulture." This time Paul seemed to wrap his tongue around it a little more comfortably.

I smiled. "To Harold and Maggie."

UNIVERSITY

Vakarovsky and I started to fill the little plot in the courtyard as soon as the weather got warmer. It was my job to go to the garden centre and buy the plants with the budget we had been given by the school. Vakarovsky told me which centre to go to and said to mention his name and they would give me the best plants. It was a little place in a run down plaza on Finch. The staff were three women with weather beaten faces and strong hands. I found out later that they were sisters. When I first went they were surly and unwelcoming; they warmed up slightly when I mentioned Vakarovsky, and directed me to take some plants from a stand in a back corner rather than the ones I had taken from the displays at the front. The oldest woman rang up my purchase and gestured towards the rejected plants with her chin. "Vladimir will give you shit if you bring those ones." I didn't like to ask why they had them at the front of the store if they were no good, so I just said thank you, paid for the plants and left.

At first we just got the hardy pansies that would survive spring snow and frost, but week by week we were able to put more into the ground and I became a regular at the garden centre. The eldest garden centre sister had injured her back lifting potted trees and since they had gotten used to me and saw that I knew something about plants, they hired me for the spring and summer without filling out an application or interviewing.

My final year of high school was coming to an end. I picked up more hours at the garden centre. My hands were always dirty. My back and legs ached from lifting heavy bags of soil and mulch. I was so tired after work that I didn't have the energy to go to Calliope with Tomasz and Shakil. Shakil would have given me a hard time about my nails (cut short to make it easier to clean dirt out) and hair (always in a messy bun full of dirt and twigs).

Exams were starting and Vakarovsky and I were working in the school plot. The afternoon sun gave the grungy courtyard a mellow, lush feel and the only sounds were of birds, and our tools as we dug in the dirt and pulled weeds.

"Do you have university acceptance yet?" Vakarovsky was crouched over a row of radishes. The red bulb or the maturing radishes could be seen at the surface of the soil. Vakarovsky expertly pulled weeds and underdeveloped radish plants to allow the maturing radishes space to grow larger.

"Yes. I got accepted to both Queen's and Guelph." Yuri had connected a long hose for us to water the plants and I unrolled it to prepare to soak the garden plot before leaving.

"Congratulations!" Vakarovsky stood and reached out a soil encrusted hand for me to shake. I laughed and offered my own muddy hand in return. "Have you decided where you will go?"

I hadn't given much thought to it, but when I got both acceptances I went back to look at the websites for both programs. The Queen's website showed wonderfully modern labs and shiny students in lab coats and safety goggles. The Guelph website had pictures of greenhouses and tree grafts. I realized that ever since spring had arrived and I had started working at the garden centre I had been bone tired, dirty and sunburnt. I was happy. The smell of dirt and plants made me feel peaceful.

"I think I will choose Guelph." I turned the hose on and the water droplets caught the light as they fell. Vakarovsky and I stood watching as the water soaked the soil and bathed the plant leaves.

Vakarovsky nodded. "Good."

*   *   *

After the bustle of moving, orientation week and settling into residence I took a breath one day in my *Introduction to Soil Chemistry* class and looked around. Every single person in that lecture hall was white. Including me, obviously. I tried to think of another time that I had been in such a large group of white people and I couldn't come up with anything.

The class was about seventy-five students. I would say that sixty of them were guys. Both the guys and the girls looked extraordinarily healthy. Many of them were on the heavy side and lots of the guys were absolutely huge with massive chests and arms. I was impossibly small and thin by comparison. An extremely sturdy girl with a ruddy complexion sat next to me. The lecture was about to start but she smiled at me. "Hi. I'm Abby." She reached out to shake my hand and enveloped my hand in hers. I thought that I had gotten strong working in the garden centre all summer, but I felt Abby could crush me with one of her hands by mistake. I tried to hold my own in the hand shake and told her my name.

After the lecture Abby and I walked out together. "You're from Toronto?" Abby was surprised. "Like actually from there?" I assured her that I was. "Wow. What was that like growing up? I've been there a few times and it is exciting, but I don't think I could live there. Isn't it dangerous?"

"No, not really..." I weighed the idea of telling her about the shooting at Bouillabaisse and then thought the better of it. We had stopped outside the lecture hall and a guy came up to talk to Abby. He was carrying a huge sports equipment bag.

"Hey sis."

"Hi Brandon. This is Frida. She's from Toronto." Abby stood back a little and held out her arm towards me like she was introducing a rare species.

Brandon was also of an imposing physique, but he was a little more lean and agile-looking than his sister. Brandon would have been extremely handsome if not for a slightly crooked nose, which, together with the equipment bag, lead me to guess that he was a hockey player.

Abby gestured towards the bag. "Have you started practices already?"

"Yep."

I looked at Brandon and I thought of Tomasz and how he always used to tell me to find "a nice Canadian boy who plays hockey." Hoping that I wouldn't sound crazy I took out my phone. "Would you guys mind if I took a picture with you to send to my friend? He wants to see who I am going to school with." Abby and Brandon agreed and he draped his arm over his sister's shoulder. She smiled broadly. I snapped the shot, said thanks, and that I had to go to my next class. I sent the picture to Tomasz with the caption

Finally found hockey player.

His reply came through right away.

got a girl already, tho
that's the sister.
see if you can get some time in the penalty box with him!

I laughed and put away my phone. I missed Tomasz.

Costanza was my roommate in residence. She was studying commerce and was extremely organized and driven. She had a white board where she put her colour-coded schedule of classes, work and volunteer hours. Her parents owned a catering company and she worked for them helping to prepare and serve food at events. She was hardly ever around and when she was there it was just to sleep and shower.

By the end of September I hadn't really found a group of people to hang out with. Abby and I had all the same classes and we would usually sit together, but she was living on her parents' farm and had to get back as soon as classes were finished so I was left to my own devices.

The weather was still mild and I started going to the Arboretum and walking around the vast gardens there. The residence dining hall was crowded and noisy, so I would grab a tuna sandwich, an apple and a big cookie and eat sitting on a bench beside an enormous oak tree.

There were lots of people enjoying the gardens, and when I had been there a few times I started to recognize a few regulars. There was an older woman with a small white dog and a pair of mothers with toddlers. The kids would chase each other around the grass while their mothers drank coffee and periodically ran after the kids when they got too far away. For a few days there was also a worker who was clearing some overgrown plants from a large area of planted beds. He worked quietly. Once or twice another worker came with a small gof cart type vehicle to take away the plant material he had cleared. He exchanged a few words with the driver, but then went straight back to work.

I wanted to offer to help him. I thought it would have been nice to feel the dirt and the satisfying give of the plants as they were pulled from the ground. I figured that wouldn't be allowed, but I watched him work. He was an older guy, maybe forty or fifty. He wore green work clothes with the University of Guelph logo, but he also wore a hat that didn't match. It was brown, with a different logo. I managed to see that the logo was the letters DFC with a black vertical lines on either side of the letters. Underneath the letters was written "Sudbury".

I looked up DFC Sudbury and found that it was a mining company. I had to go to class, but that hat and that logo were stuck in my head and I had a hard time focusing on the lecture. It seemed so familiar, and the reason it was familiar was in a background part of my brain, further back than the thoughts of everyday life: classes and laundry and what was going to be for dinner, further back than Alex and Vivian, Tomasz and Shakil, further back even than Sandra and Thorton Middle School.

When I got to my dorm room, Costanza was there. "Hey Frida! Wow, seems like I never see you! How's it going?" Costanza had done a load of laundry and was folding t-shirts. She laid them out on the bed and folded them briskly into perfect rectangles.

"You're so busy Costanza." I gestured to her whiteboard, "Do you even stop to eat?"

"Oh I usually just eat whatever food we are preparing for catering. There's always enough to go around." Costanza had finished the t-shirts and started on her jeans.

"I used to work in a restaurant. The chef would feed us great stuff." I hadn't thought about Bouillabaisse in a long time, but I smiled now to remember how Francois used to try and school us on French cuisine and be horrified at our ignorance.

"I didn't know you had restaurant experience!" Costanza was clearly impressed. "Would you ever want some catering work? We always need people."

"Sure. I could use the money and I don't seem to have much of a social life here."

"Great! I'll let you know."

Costanza finished folding her laundry and then dashed off. I studied for a while and then took a nap. I must have slept soundly because it was dark when I woke up. I sat up in bed. I realized why that hat was familiar. I went into my closet and took out the envelope of pictures from Arlene that I had brought with me from home. I took out the pictures and looked for the ones taken by the lake. It didn't take me long to find the one. Someone giving a toast with Arlene sitting behind him. My Dad was there, leaning over to say something to Arlene. He wore a brown hat with the DFC Sudbury logo. I sat looking at the photo for a long time.

The next day I went back to the Arboretum. I wasn't sure if I would try to talk to the worker in the DFC Sudbury hat or just try to get a good look at him. The bed that he had been working on for the past few days was all cleaned up. He wasn't there. For the next week I went to a different part of the Arboretum every day to see if I could find him. Each area of the Arboretum had a different vibe. There were wooded areas with walking trails, areas with collections of different types of trees: a birch tree area and a lilac tree area. There was a Japanese style garden that you entered by going through a wooden gate and then crossing a low stone bridge. There was an English garden and an Italian garden with low hedges immaculately trimmed and laid out to form the structure of the garden. In the Italian garden there was also a fountain and, on the eighth day of searching the various areas for the worker, I sat on a bench near this fountain. The weather was still warm even though it was October. The warmth of the sun and the gurgling of the fountain made me drowsy and I closed my eyes. With my eyes closed the sounds of the garden were more pronounced. I could hear the crunch of gravel when people walked by on the path. There were layers of birdsong: some from birds close by and some from birds that were further away. I could hear dogs, the clink of their leashes and their snuffling sounds as they investigated beneath hedges or other passing dogs.

Amongst the other sounds I also heard a metallic clipping accompanied by rustling that seemed to be coming from the other side of the large hedge that encircled the fountain area. I listened to the clip and rustle sound for a minute and then I thought that it must be someone pruning the hedge. I opened my eyes and got up to investigate. Sure enough someone was pruning the hedge, clipping and shaking out the branches to create the desired shape. It was the worker in the brown DFC Sudbury hat. He worked intently and didn't notice me at first. I looked at the side of his face under the hat. He had a bit of a beard, but I could see his cheekbones clearly. They were prominent, like mine. Like the guy in the picture.

Eventually he realized that I was watching him and he paused his work to look at me. Up close and facing me full on I could see the guy who was in the picture with Arlene. I was nervous, but glad that I had found him. There was only one thing to do.

"Are you Luke?"

He held the clippers in one hand and looked at me carefully. He took the glove off the hand that wasn't holding the clippers by holding the tip of the middle finger in his teeth and pulling his hand out. He used this newly ungloved hand to wipe sweat from his face.

"Do I know you?" He said in a wondering tone like he know me somewhere in the back of his mind, but he couldn't remember who I was.

"I'm Frida." I paused to let this sink in.

"Frida?" He tilted his head to the side and looked at me questioningly.

"I think you're my Dad."

LUKE (DAD)

A wealthy alumnus of the university had made a big donation to renovate and upgrade some facilities in the Health Sciences building. There was a reception planned for the dignitaries of the university, the donor, and some faculty members to celebrate the new facilities and unveil a plaque recognizing the donation. Costanza's parents were catering the reception and she asked me whether I could work prep and the reception on Saturday night.

"My cousin Joey is supposed to be working too, but half the time he doesn't show up and when he does he drinks more than he serves."

I told Costanza I could work. It was exam time and I had missed a few classes since that day in the Italian garden. It was hard to concentrate when I was trying to come to terms with meeting Luke and with everything he had told me. It didn't help that I was hitting the whiskey bottle pretty hard to get to sleep. Early morning classes were painful. One day, Abby sat beside me and wrinkled her nose. "Jeez, Frida. You smell like booze. It's Tuesday morning."

My head was pounding and I couldn't think of anything to say so I just nodded. "Bit of a rough night." Abby started sitting in a different part of the lecture hall after that. I didn't know whether I was sad or relieved.

The health sciences reception was the last Friday before exams finished for Christmas break. I had my soil chemistry exam at eleven and then I was going to go to the caterer to help out with prep and the reception was to start at six. I had done well the night before, the whiskey bottle was empty and I didn't buy a fresh one. I put the bottle in the small grey trash can I had bought at the dollar store with Maggie when I first moved into residence. Seeing that little trash can made me think of Maggie. I imagined the disappointed look she would get on her face if she could see me. I crumpled up some paper to cover the empty bottle so that if you looked at the trash can it looked like one belonging to a a hard-studying university student, not a hard-drinking one.

The exam was difficult. Especially the questions about the material we had covered in the past month when I had been either absent or hung over. When I had answered as many questions as I could there was still loads of time left. Everyone else was still working intently. There was one question about typical Ontario soil types. I had written as much as I could, but the question reminded me of Luke. "One thing about that Stouffville house, though. The soil was great for planting. We never had soil like that in Sudbury."

Luke hadn't reacted strongly when I first told him that I thought he was my father.

"I think you are my Dad."

He looked at me silently for a minute, squinting a little in the sunshine. "I can see you've got Arlene's eyes." Luke's co-worker with the golf cart had arrived just then. Luke gestured towards the hedge. "Look, I gotta finish up here."

"Okay. Can we meet up later? When you are finished work?"

The golf cart driving co-worker was looking at us with curiosity, but she didn't say anything. "Sure. I'm done at four. I'll meet you here."

I went back to my dorm room to get the pictures so I could show them to Luke. I sat on my bed looking at them and trying to prepare what I would say to him. What would I ask him? I considered not going back to the garden. Maybe it would be easier to just forget the whole thing. I had got along fine without him for all these years. Why was I trying to know him now?

I kept looking at the two pictures: the one with someone giving a toast and Arlene and Luke in the background, that was the one where he was wearing the DFC Sudbury hat, and the one of the three of us at Sauble Beach. I looked at my baby self and Arlene and tried to see if we had the same eyes like Luke had said. I couldn't really tell. Arlene looked so young. I wondered how old she was when she had me. I realized that she could have been not much older than me in that picture. I tried to imagine myself with a baby and I couldn't.

I stood up and looked at myself in the full length mirror that Costanza had hung near her bed. I looked like a child, someone could easily guess me to be twelve years old. My hair was in the same style I had kept it in since Sandra suggested that bangs would look good on me. I was still stick thin with only minimal breasts and hips. I always wore jeans and a sweatshirt. The one I had then I had won during orientation week. It was yellow with a Guelph Gryphons logo. It was too big for me which made me look even smaller. I took the sweatshirt off and looked at myself in just a tank top. In the Sauble Beach picture, Arlene was thin too, but she had more boobs. Her hair was cut with no bangs and she had it in a braid that came to the side and down over one shoulder. I borrowed a hair band from Costanza's dresser and pulled my bangs back under it. I tried to braid my hair in the same style as Arlene, with some success. I took two pairs of rolled up socks and stuffed them into my tank top for fake boobs. I compared myself again to the picture. There was a similarity, I thought. With my bangs pulled back, my eyes looked more like Arlene's. Arlene's face was pink from the sun in the picture and my skin had a similar colour from being out in the garden all day trying to find Luke.

They looked happy in that Sauble Beach picture. What had happened? How did they go from the Sauble Beach couple to where Arlene let me wander off into a snowy field in my diaper and Luke "fucked off back up North"? Maybe I had been a really bad kid and they couldn't handle me. Maggie had always said it was nothing to do with me, that my parents had their own problems. But maybe she had just said that to make me feel better about myself.

Would Luke be able to tell me what had happened? It was almost four. I took the braid and the socks out, but I kept my bangs pulled back. I put the two pictures inside a binder in my backpack and when back to the Arboretum to meet my father.

Luke had no small talk. When we sat on the bench by the fountain at four o'clock I showed him the two pictures. He didn't say anything and I found the silence too awkward. I pointed to one of the pictures. "I recognized the hat."

Luke nodded. "They used to give out tons of those hats. I swear every guy in Sudbury's got two or three in his closet."

"Is that where you're from, Sudbury?"

"Yep."

"Was Mom from there too?"

Luke looked a little surprised. "Arlene? From Sudbury? No. She was from Toronto."

I could see that this wasn't going to be easy. I wanted the whole story laid out clearly for me so I could fill in my own blanks, but Luke was not telling any stories that day. He handed the pictures back to me. "I gotta go eat something now. I been working all day."

I put the pictures back in my backpack. "Okay"

Luke stood up with a groan and put his hands on the small of his back. "Hedge pruning always does a number on my back, eh?"

I made what I hoped was a sympathetic noise. Was he going to take off now, I wondered, and I'd have to stalk him all over the Arboretum again if I wanted to talk to him? Luke put his hands in his pockets and shifted from one foot to the other. I waited.

He cleared his throat. "Thanks for bringing those pictures to show me."

"Yeah. You're welcome."

He rubbed his face with his hand. "I guess I might have some pictures around somewhere too. If you'd like to see 'em."

"Sure. I'd like that."

"Okay then. I'll give you my number."

I pulled out my phone. He gave me his number. I set up his contact as "Luke (Dad)".

It took me a few weeks to get up the nerve to call him, but finally I did and we agreed to meet up for a late breakfast at a diner near the university. I arrived first and I saw Luke pull up in a rusty Dodge Caravan. Did he have a new family? I wondered. He walked a little gingerly to the diner and when he sat down I could see that his eyes were red and his skin was blotchy. He smelled of stale cigarette smoke. He wore crumpled beige cargo pants and his shirt was worn at the cuffs. He didn't have his hat on and it looked like he had made some effort to wet and comb his thinning brown hair. Although it was difficult to see the handsome, tanned young man from the Sauble Beach picture, Luke still had the prominent cheek bones and thin, wiry body.

We ordered coffee and breakfast and sat in awkward silence for a few minutes. Luke cleared his throat and rubbed his face with his hand. He reached into his back pocket and pulled out his wallet. From inside the wallet he pulled out a picture that was worn around the edges. I could tell he had been carrying it in that wallet for a long time.

The picture was of a group of girls in a bar, but it had been cut so that you could only see the whole of one of the girls, the others, who were sitting on either side were cut off so that you could only see an arm and shoulder of one and half a head and chest of the other. The picture quality wasn't very good, it had been taken with a flash in a dark bar. Luke put his finger on the central figure in the picture. "That's Arlene. That's your mom when I first knew her." She was smiling broadly in the picture. She had her hair in that side braid like in the Sauble Beach picture, but in this picture she was more made up and she looked older. She had a drink in one hand and a cigarette in the other.

"How did you meet?" I handed Luke back the picture and he put in back in his wallet.

"I came down to Toronto to look for work and I used to go to this bar on Gerrard, it was called the Red Robin Tap and Grill. Arlene worked there. That's how we met."

I nodded. Our food arrived and we ate silently. Luke bent over his plate and ate with concentration. He ate his way through the breakfast item by item: eggs, then sausage, then toast. He cleared his plate of every crumb and then pushed it away slightly and said "Hm, good" almost to himself.

I had finished about half of my food then asked for more coffee. "What was she like?"

Luke looked out the window of the diner and rubbed his face with his hand. "Hard to describe. You would never forget her once you met her. I remember the first time I seen her. She was working behind the bar and men were fallin' all over themselves to get her attention. She would just serve their drinks and laugh them off when they came on to her. 'You're too old for me' she would say, or 'I heard you use that same line with Crystal the other day.'" Luke smiled at this memory. "It was hard to get to know her really because she would just joke around and she was always moving, serving the drinks, cleaning up the bar and the tables. On her break she would run to out to buy cigarettes and a sandwich from the Italian bakery. I almost never saw her sit down."

"How did you two get together?"

"I guess she kind of chose me." Luke said this with wonder, like he wasn't sure how it had happened. "I never made a move on her 'cuz I seen how she shut down them other guys and I figured I didn't have a chance. But one night she came on to me. It was quick, like everything she did. Before I knew what hit me we were living together and she was pregnant with you."

"Was she happy to be pregnant, or was it, like, a mistake?"

Luke considered this for a minute. "She was suprised. She told me that she couldn't have babies. She was pretty far along before we found out. She hardly looked pregnant until the very end and then her belly just popped out. You were born a couple of weeks early."

"Was she scared?"

"I don't think so. She didn't have her mom anymore and she never had any sisters or girlfriends with kids to tell her stories and get her going about how hard it was."

She must have been scared, I thought. How could you not be? "What happened to her mom?"

Luke got a pained looked on his face. "That's a sad story, Frida."

Our coffee had gotten cold and there were people waiting for a table. "Why don't we get out of here and go for a walk?"

Luke agreed. He paid for our food and we left the diner.

The weather had cooled off. Almost all the leaves were gone from the trees and it felt like it could snow at any minute. I wrapped my scarf tightly around my neck and jumped from foot to foot a little to warm up. Luke was wearing a flannel shirt and a grey windbreaker type jacket, but he didn't seem to be cold. He lit a cigarette and we walked together along Gordon Street towards the covered bridge. We didn't say much of anything until we got to the bridge. We stopped and leaned our elbows on the railing so we could look at the water. The few people who were out walking or biking would make the wooden bridge rattle as they passed. Luke kept looking at the water as he told me what had happened to Arlene's mom.

"Arlene lived with her mom in an old house off Coxwell Avenue. The house had belonged to her mom's family but they hadn't kept it up too well. They didn't have much money. Arlene's dad was a deadbeat, he was never around. To try and make some money Arlene's mom rented out rooms in the basement and the main floor."

The wind was picking up now and I was getting cold standing still, but I didn't want to interrupt Luke. I got the sense that it was hard for him to talk so much.

"Yeah, so one night one of the renters fell asleep while smoking a cigarette. The whole place went up in flames. Arlene was only five years old, her mom wrapped her in a blanket and threw her out the window. She was the only one who survived. A neighbour smelled the smoke, came out to see what was going on and heard Arlene crying from inside the blanket in a bush in the front yard."

"Holy shit."

"Yeah. I think that really messed Arlene up. She never really had a family after that, just foster care and group homes and shit."

Luke didn't have anything more to say. We walked back to where he had parked and said goodbye. That night in my room I couldn't stop thinking about Arlene, how tough it must have been to lose her mom like that. I wondered if she had been a good mom before the fire, my Grandmother. I tried to imagine her. She had been so brave to throw Arlene out the window like that. I drank from my whiskey bottle and fell asleep in my clothes. I dreamed that Arlene and Luke were trying to put out a fire by throwing liquid at it. But the liquid was alcohol so the fire just blazed up and burned more fiercely.

*   *   *

Costanza's parents had a unit in an industrial building where they would prep for events. I left my soil chemistry exam as soon as I could without making it obvious that I hadn't answered at least half of the questions. I arrived at the prep kitchen an hour earlier than I said I would be there. It was so different from the cramped kitchen at Bouillabaisse where Francois had presided. This was a large, open space with big stainless steel tables in addition to the ovens, fridges and stoves where two cooks in whites worked to turn out the various dishes. Unlike the restaurant, the food was not going to be served immediately. It was our job, Costanza, Joey (if he showed up) and me, to help with basic prep and then pack up the prepared items in trays and bins so that they could be transported to the site of the reception where one cook would come to do final prep and check the food before it went out to the guests. They were also prepping for another event the following night and the white board with assigned tasks looked as complex as I imagined planning for a military invasion would look.

"Thank God you're here, Frida." Costanza face was tight with stress. "We're way behind and of course Joey hasn't shown up." Costanza put me to work prepping satay skewers that would be grilled and handed around with a peanut dipping sauce. She was working chopping tomatoes, onions and peppers that were going to top small pieces of toasted bread as crostini. Costanza started to relax when she saw that I knew how to work. I moved quickly through the bowl of marinated meat and the pile of prepared skewers grew quickly on the platter in front of me.

"My fucking cousin. He pisses me off so much, you know?" Costanza chopped her vegetables with precision and a little more energy then was absolutely necessary, but it was definitely an outlet for her anger at her cousin. "And you know, he'll turn up eventually and he'll have some wild excuse and he'll be all charming and funny and I won't be able to stay mad at him."

I didn't have much to say since I didn't know the cousin or even Costanza that well, so I just mumbled something vague. "I'm sure that must be annoying," and kept on with my skewers.

"He wasn't always like this, you know? He was always the cutest, nicest guy and we got along great. Then he started dating some white trash girl ..." here Costanza paused for a beat and looked at me sideways. I didn't stop what I was doing or look back at her. "She was this real trashy slut that he met at some club and she turned him onto drugs. They broke up, but he keeps using. He says it is just for fun and he has it under control, but he's not the same guy anymore, you know?"

I felt a little awkward listening to all this, but obviously Costanza needed to get it off her chest. She had finished chopping a big bowl of crostini topping and leaned against the table for a minute, flexing her arm and stretching her knife hand. "I've tried talking to him, but it's like he's not there. It's not Joey anymore." This was almost exactly what Luke had said about Arlene.

After the day by the covered bridge, I didn't hear from Luke for a while. Classes were becoming more stressful because final exams were coming up. I hadn't done well on most of my midterms and labs, but if I did well on the finals I would probably pass. I didn't share any of this with Harold and Maggie. I just said I was busy, busy, having a great time, lots of studying and meeting new people. I think Maggie suspected that everything was not okay. "You look a little pale, Frida. Are you eating enough meat?" I told her I was fine, it was just the lighting on the video call that made me look pale. "Okay, well, we will get you nice and healthy when you come home for Christmas." I had to make an excuse to hang up the call so that I wouldn't cry.

The whiskey bottle was where I turned most days and I was walking home from the LCBO with a new bottle when I ran into Luke. "What's your poison?" Luke gestured towards the brown paper bag. He was surprised when he saw the whiskey. I knew it was unusual for a girl my age to drink whiskey, but the sweet mixed drinks and ciders that I saw the other girls drinking did not give me the same satisfying burn followed by warm numbness that I had come to rely on. Luke looked at the whiskey bottle with fondness.

Even though I had class in an hour, I asked Luke if he wanted to have a drink together. He considered this for a minute and rubbed his face with his hand. "There's an office at the vet school where no one ever goes. One of the guys on my crew slept there for a month when he split up with his wife." I agreed that this sounded like a good spot and we headed over there. Luke told me that he only worked a couple of days a week for the university in the winter.

We got a couple of paper cups from the coffee shop across the road from the vet school. The building was impressive, but we didn't go in through the showy front doors and enormous foyer. Instead, Luke led the way around back to the loading dock. There were a bunch of garbage dumpsters there and the smell of those combined with the smell of diesel cut through the fresh cold air. There was one security guard looking at his phone. He lifted his head only slightly when we walked by.

Luke waved at him casually, "How's it going, buddy?" and the security guard went back to looking at his phone.

The "office" was more like a storage area with a bunch of boxes, an old couch (I figured this is where Luke's co-worker must have slept), a desk with a dusty old computer monitor and a couple of old office chairs, one with a broken arm rest and the other missing a wheeled foot. Luke sat on the couch and I sat o the chair with the broken arm rest. I opened the whiskey bottle and poured for the two of us. It didn't take long for the whiskey to loosen Luke's tongue.

"Arlene had no idea how to take care of a baby. She wouldn't do the whole breast-feeding thing and if it hadn't of been for the public health nurse telling her how to get the special baby formula explaining how to make it, I don't what she would of fed you. But Arlene really liked that nurse, she was this fat German lady that just told Arlene what to do and Arlene did what she said. I think she was a little afraid of that nurse.

"Eventually she got pretty good at it and you got bigger and I was working steady with landscaping. That Sauble Beach picture is from that time. We were doing so good. I don't why it went all to shit. Arlene started to say that she missed her friends from work and she would leave you with the neighbour and go over to the Red Robin in the afternoon. At first, it was just when you were napping, but then she started staying there longer and longer. One day I come home late from working a big job and Arlene had been gone all afternoon. The neighbour was a real nice lady but she had her own kids and couldn't take care of you all the time. So Arlene started taking you along in the stroller and she would sit out on the patio with you and drink and smoke and laugh with her friends from the bar." Luke held out his cup for a refill.

"So one day I go there all pissed off 'cuz I know it's not cool for a baby to be in that kind of place all the time. I arrive and I seen Arlene sitting with this guy Nick who used to always hit on her when she worked behind the bar. So I am really pissed off now and I can see that she's drunk and Nick's eyeing her and you're sitting in a wet diaper, so I tell her 'Come on, Arlene. It's time to go home.' Well. Fucking Nick pipes up, 'She don't have to go if she don't want to.' He puts his hand on her wrist." Luke was getting agitated telling this story and he got up off the couch and started pacing up and down the room.

"I see red and I tell him, 'Take your hands off her!' He was a big prick. He used to work construction until he injured his leg, but he was still big. He stands up and gets in my face. 'Who's gonna make me? You?'

"I mighta just walked away if it hadna been for Arlene sitting there. She didn't say nothing. She just sat watching like we were entertainment. I grabbed a flower pot off of one of the tables and smashed him in the head with it. He musta been drinking a fair bit because he didn't react hardly at all. He just kinda stumbled and touched his hand to his head where I had hit him. He looked at his hand and saw blood and then he came at me. By that time other people seen what was going on and they held him back." Luke flopped back down to the couch and rubbed his face with his hand. "Stupid fucking prick. Why didn't he just keep his mouth shut?"

My class was due to start in ten minutes. If I didn't leave I would miss it, but I didn't know when I would see Luke again and have him in this talkative mood. I decided to stay. "So what happened then?" Luke looked at me, a little confused, like he had forgotten I was there, or had forgotten who I was. He took another swig of whiskey and held out his cup for a refill.

"The owner of the Red Robin had been getting a lot of heat from the neighbours over their customers being too rowdy, so I guess he kinda wanted to send a message that he wasn't gonna put up with fighting on his patio. He called the cops and made his employees give witness statements and told Nick he better do the same or he wouldn't be welcome there. So, long story short, I got charged with assault causing bodily harm and my lawyer made a deal to get the charge reduced to assault and I only had to serve six months, but that's where I was on your first birthday. In jail."

"Shit." I felt bad for Luke. Obviously he shouldn't have hit that guy over the head with a flowerpot, but he deserved it in a way.

"Yeah, so that's when Arlene moved up to Stouffville. She couldn't afford to stay in our Toronto apartment without my paycheque and her friends at the Red Robin and the neighbour started giving her the cold shoulder after the whole thing. She didn't have nothing to stick around for. She had this real loser friend from high school whose Grandma had died and left the Stouffville house empty. It might of been nice at one time, but when Arlene went to live there it was just a party house where a bunch of people crashed regularly and a bunch more would come by on weekends to party. Arlene had her baby bonus money coming in so she could pay for booze or weed or whatever. She took you and went up there."

"I remember that house."

Luke looked at the floor and rubbed his face with his hand. "It was no place for a baby. You were just this sweet, innocent thing in the middle of all that. When I got out of jail I went straight there thinking I would just collect you guys and we would leave. But Arlene was different. She had started using drugs and she couldn't think of nothing else. I tried to talk to her, but it was like she wasn't even the same person." Luke looked at me with a pleading look, like he wanted me to understand. He had downed a fair bit of whiskey by now and his words were getting a bit slurred. "I'm sorry, Frida. I didn't know what to do and I knew I couldn't take care of you. I couldn't stand seeing Arlene like that and I figured I would end up beating up one of the other assholes that lived there and that woulda landed me in jail cuz I was on proma... promotion... no.

Probation." Luke made an effort to get the word out. He leaned his head against the back of the couch like it was too heavy for him to hold up. He was quiet for a minute and then I realized that he had fallen asleep.

I got up quietly and found a ratty blanket to cover him. I left the whiskey bottle on the desk where I hoped he would see it and I left.

JOEY

Costanza was right, Joey did show up eventually. We were almost done packing and prepping the trays and bins when he came in.

"Holy fuck! It smells like heaven in here! How do you geniuses make something smell so good?" he didn't slink in apologetically. He came through the door like he was arriving at a party being thrown for him. Costanza had said that he would be funny and charming, but she had failed to mention that he was also gorgeous. He had dark, curly hair and brown eyes with impossible eyelashes. He was beautiful and possessed of an electric energy that drew me in so totally I realized my mouth was open and Costanza was looking at me with disdain. He swooped in and started carrying the prepared trays and bins to the van. Time was tight now. The event was due to start in just over an hour.

After the van was loaded Costanza, Joey and I squeezed into the front seat. Costanza was driving, I was in the middle and Joey sat by the window. "Who is this slender lovely?" Joey smiled at me as we set off for the university.

"Joey, this is Frida. She's my roommate at school." Costanza turned out of the industrial area onto the main road. "And the newest member of your fan club, looks like.'

"Aw, cugina, don't be jealous. You know you'll always be president of my fan club." Joey winked at me.

"In your dreams, asshole." Costanza tried to sound mad, but I could tell she wasn't. Joey connected his phone to the van's sound system and played "Sicko Mode". It felt a little weird listening to that music driving through the streets of Guelph, but I didn't say anything.

The venue for the event was beautiful. The sciences complex took up a whole city block across from Johnston Green. Costanza had to drive around the complex a few times before she found the right entrance. Joey was energized and worked well bringing the food into the small kitchen where the cook would do the final prep before we served the food and drinks. The cook arrived soon after us with his wife who would help us out with serving. She was a professional. When she took off her hat and jacket and I saw her blonde hair pulled tightly back and her immaculately clean and pressed white shirt and black pants I had a strong wave of nostalgia for Bouillabaisse, for Sandra and for Tomasz. I sent Tomasz a selfie with the busy kitchen in the background.

Can't escape food service.

I managed to capture Joey in the shot too and Tomasz responded

Who's the gorgeous boy?

I sent a blushing emoji and put my phone away. Guests were starting to arrive.

The reception was being held in the atrium of the health sciences building. It was a massive space with a big staircase that connected the main floor where you entered to the second floor where you could access classrooms and labs and faculty offices. There was classical music playing and a large monitor showing a video of the newly renovated labs and a montage of pictures of the donor and his family. He was a white-haired guy who was shown in the video wearing an expensive looking suit and a tie with a bright green geometric pattern. The tie was a little splashy and I wondered if his wife or daughter had told him to wear it. I tried to picture Luke wearing a tie of any sort and I couldn't. Harold wore a tie quite regularly, but never anything flashy. I hadn't told Harold and Maggie about meeting Luke. I hadn't told anyone. The person I really wanted to tell, who I thought would understand how messed up I felt about meeting him and hearing about why he left and about Arlene, the only person I wanted to share all that with was Sandra. I hadn't thought about her too much since coming to Guelph, but now I missed her so much it hurt. When I saw Joey sneak a bottle of vodka out of the bar cart and take it into the small seminar room that had been converted into a coat check, I followed him.

The coat check room was quieter than the open space of the atrium where people's voices were getting louder the more they drank. The coats were hanging on portable racks. They were mainly dark grey or black, but there was one white one with a fur collar. I'm pretty sure it was fake fur, but it felt wonderfully soft. The white coast still held the scent of its owner's perfume, and I breathed this in with closed eyes.

"Why don't you try it on?" Joey had been watching me sniff and caress the white coat. He was looking at me while holding the vodka bottle casually against his thigh. I wasn't sure what I wanted more, Joey or the bottle, but I tried to play it cool. I took the white coat off its hanger and pulled it on. Its owner must have been a very small woman, because it fit me well. I turned the collar up so that the fur framed my face.

"How does it look?"

Joey smiled. He handed me the bottle. I took a drink from it. "Let me get a shot of you." He took out his phone. I didn't have time to pose. Joey looked at the shot. "Wow." He put his arm around my shoulder and showed me the picture he had taken. It was a bit blurry, I guess I had moved. I looked like an actress from an old movie, mysterious and beautiful.

"Well. Look at me." I took another drink from the bottle.

Joey put his face next to mine and took a picture of the two of us. "You're alright, Costanza's roommate." He helped me take the coat off and we hid the bottle in the dark back corner of the room.

In some ways, serving food at an event like that one was much easier than Bouillabaisse. Everyone got offered the same thing. If they didn't want it, they didn't take it. There was a lot more walking around though, and my feet were definitely getting tired. Every so often I would sneak into the coat check room to drink. The vodka and the buzz of people's voices and the looks that Joey would give me when our paths crossed all combined to make me feel lighter than air.

After the rich donor gave his speech and most of the food and drink was gone, the crowd thinned out quickly. Some people had taken their glasses and plates upstairs and Costanza sent me up to gather them. Joey had commandeered the sound system and had put on dance music. I wanted to go to a dance club with him and press up against him on a crowded dance floor. From the second floor window I looked out onto a driveway at the side of the building. I could see that Joey was standing there under a streetlight talking to a guy with a receding hairline in a black bomber jacket. The guy in the bomber jacket handed a small packet to Joey and they did a handshake hug thing. I knew that this was his dealer. He had just scored. Seeing this didn't turn me off Joey. I didn't want him to think that I wasn't cool. "You're alright," he had told me. I wanted that approval.

I gathered up as many of the plates and glasses as I could fit on my tray and carried them down. There were still a couple of glasses, but I would have to come back for those. Joey was talking with Costanza in the kitchen when I brought in the tray of plates and glasses. Costanza was annoyed. I figured she had seen him go out to meet his dealer too. She saw me loading the dirty plates into the bin. "Is that all of them?"

"No. There's just a couple more upstairs. I'll go grab them now." I had drunk a fair bit of the coat check vodka and I hadn't eaten much – just a couple of satay skewers. I didn't want Costanza to know that I had been drinking, so I worked hard to act straight. Joey watched me try to pull off this act with a conspiratorial smirk.

"I'll go help out. Just check to make sure we got 'em all." He took me by the elbow and we out of the kitchen together. As soon as we were out of ear shot, we started laughing and falling into one another. "Oh yes, boss ... I'll go grab those glasses right away!" Joey imitated me trying to sound sober and efficient.

"Shut up!" I gave him a playful shove. "You're one to talk! Mr. 'sneak off to meet my dealer.'"

Joey stopped laughing. "What are you talking about?"

I tried to keep the tone light. We were on our way up the stairs now and I sped up a little and got in front of him. "I saw you out the window." I wagged my finger at him with a 'naughty boy' gesture.

He looked at me for a minute, but then he smiled and my legs felt like they really might give way. But they didn't. I got to the top of the stairs, grabbed the last two glasses and turned to head down. Joey had stopped three quarters of the way up and when he saw me coming down again he turned around, hopped up on the handrail and slid gracefully down. He looked up at me from the bottom of the stairs. "C'mon, Costanza's roommate. Almost quitting time!"

I felt sure we were going to go somewhere together when this job was finished. I could feel my heart beating and my head felt light. I looked at the hand rail. I put both glasses into my left hand and used my right hand to hoist myself up onto the smooth, polished handrail. I could feel myself start to slide. I held my left hand with the glasses out, and I lifted my feet away from the railing to reduce friction. I started to pick up speed and my stomach lurched as I gained momentum down the handrail. I slid for about fifteen steps before losing my balance. The glasses flew out of my hand as I tried to break my fall, I heard them shatter and I heard the sickening crunch as my left wrist met the staircase. I tumbled down the remaining stairs, landing in a twisted lump at Joey's feet at the bottom.

"Oh shit!" Joey bent over me. "Are you okay?" He looked really worried. I tried to sit up. Everything hurt. He helped me and I immediately knew I was going to throw up. There was nothing I could do. I puked all over his arm and my leg and the floor. "Oh shit." Joey sounded disgusted. "Costanza!" He shouted for his cousin who came hurrying from the kitchen.

"Frida! What the hell?!" She looked equal parts scared and mad. She shot Joey a look as if to say "I know this is your fault."

"She fell down the stairs!"

Costanza ignored him. "Okay, Frida, just hang on, we're going to get you taken care of."

Campus security showed up at that moment. The event was supposed to be done by then and they were coming to lock up. When they saw me they radioed for the campus first response team. About ten minutes later three students in paramedic type gear showed up. One girl, who couldn't have been much older than me, came over. "Hi, I'm Aaliyah. I'm a trained first responder. How are you doing?"

I was sitting in a pool of my own vomit with a quickly swelling wrist and pounding head, so I just said "Not great."

She smiled. "Yeah. I can see you had a bit of a fall." She proceeded to ask me a bunch of questions and take my pulse. She was nice and even though I must have looked like a complete fool, she didn't act too judgy. I looked at her. She was bright-eyed and spoke crisply. Her long black hair was braided neatly and her slender hands were steady and sure. Why was I such a mess? Aaliyah would never fall down some stairs to impress a random dude she had just met, I was sure. She was probably going to go to med school and be a doctor and cure cancer and I was not sure I had passed a single one of my first semester courses. I felt like I was sinking into a deep, dark pit. What would I tell Harold and Maggie?

BACK HOME

Even though I had only been gone for a few months coming home to Harold and Maggie felt strange. Harold had put on weight. He seemed soft and pale and squishy. Maggie fussed over my broken wrist. She insisted on taking me to our family doctor who patiently told me exactly what the doctor at the hospital in Guelph had told me. I had given a plausible story about being tired at the end of a night working and just missing my footing on the way down the stairs. If they suspected that there was anything else to the story, they didn't say.

I spent most of my time in my room. Tomasz wanted me to come for brunch or for a night at Calliope, but I just didn't feel up to it. Vivian and Andreas were both working tons of hours to save up for first and last month's rent. They had a lead on an apartment that was going to be available in April, and they hoped to move in together then.

I did emerge one day from my room. It had snowed the night before and I put my coat on to go out into the soft whiteness.

It was mid-morning and the street was quiet. I closed my eyes and stood for a minute breathing in the cold. My mind still churned with thoughts of Luke and Arlene, Joey and Costanza and, especially now that I was home, I thought often of Sandra. Faintly I heard the crunch of approaching footsteps in the snow. I thought it might be someone walking their dog, but the steps were a little too quick. I opened my eyes and looked down the street. The approaching footsteps belonged to a young guy in a uniform wearing a bright orange safety vest and headphones. Canada Post. I hardly ever got snail mail. I hadn't even checked my e-mail since falling down the stairs. So I was surprised to see my name on the envelope the letter carrier handed to me along with a bunch of junk mail. It was definitely addressed to me, and it was from the University of Guelph.

I had a bad feeling about what might be in that letter. I tucked it into my coat pocket and took the rest of the mail in and laid it on the kitchen island where Harold and Maggie were sure to see it when they got home.

I took the University of Guelph letter upstairs to my room. My bad feeling proved correct. I had failed four out of five courses and the incident at the reception had gone on my record as "conduct contrary to student code of behaviour, actions constituting a risk to safety." I was on academic suspension and they wanted me to enrol in a non-credit post-secondary readiness course in order to consider allowing me to take credit courses again. I sat on my bed looking at the letter. My broken wrist throbbed slightly. My head ached. After a few minutes I heard a knock at the door. Figuring it was probably a package being delivered, I went downstairs to open up. Porch piracy was rampant in the neighbourhood, Maggie had told me, so I didn't want to take a chance.

I opened the door. Standing on my porch in the cold was Sandra. I was dumbfounded. She shifted her weight from one foot to the other and gave me a half smile. Sandra looked different. It was her: the dark eyes and thick hair. But her regular features were blurred somehow. Her face was bloated and her skin had a strange uneven texture. As soon as she came in the house I could smell her. A sour unwashed smell that made me reach to cover my mouth and nose without thinking.

"I must reek." Sandra saw my reaction.

There was no point denying it. "Sandra, what the hell?"

"Listen, I have a lot to tell you, but first, do you have anything to eat?"

Maggie had ordered Thai food the night before and there were leftovers in the fridge. I warmed them up for Sandra and she ate them all without pausing. While she was eating I got some clean clothes and a towel. I just handed them to her. "You remember where the bathroom is?" She nodded and went upstairs to take a shower.

I paced around the house listening to the water run. I was so happy to see her, but it was strange to see her like that. I hoped that she would emerge from the bathroom the old version of Sandra. She was cleaner when she came out. I took the clothes she had been wearing and put them in the washing machine. We went into my room. She sat on the bed and I sat on my desk chair.

"I guess you're pretty surprised to see me." Sandra gave another half smile like the one she had given at the door.

"I'm so happy to see you. I think about you all the time." As I said this, the many months of loneliness and the pain of our separation flooded over me and I started to cry.

"I think about you too, Frida." Sandra wasn't crying, but she was moved. There was something aside from our separation and reunion that was pressing more urgently on her mind. She wasn't prepared for a sobbing embrace.

"Things have just been so messed up, you know?" Sandra laid her head back on my pillows and covered her eyes with her arm.

"Why? What's been going on?"

Sandra moved her arm and looked at me. "Maybe I shouldn't have come here. You shouldn't get involved. Everything is probably going great for you. You're at university?"

I nodded.

"You got a boyfriend?"

I shook my head.

Sandra looked me up and down. "What happened to your arm?"

I realized that for Sandra, it was important that I tell the real story, not the sanitized version I had given to Harold and Maggie. "I was drunk and trying to impress a guy. I fell down some stairs."

This confession made Sandra smile her full smile. "And was he impressed?"

"Not so much, especially since I proceeded to throw up on him." We looked at each other for a minute and then started to laugh. We laughed until tears ran down our cheeks and we couldn't breathe.

"Wow, Frida," Sandra wiped her eyes with my pillowcase, "you're a mess."

"What about you?" I figured Sandra would feel better about telling me what was going on with her now that she knew I wasn't living the dream life that would be derailed by her information. She looked up at the ceiling and started to talk.

"After Carly's funeral I moved in with Amir. My mom needed to go home to Newfoundland because her dad was sick and needed someone to look after him. She wanted me to go with her, but that wasn't going to happen. I didn't want to be trapped in some shitty town where I knew no one. She told me that she would send me money and that she would come back as soon as she could.

"Fucking Amir turned out to be a real asshole. As soon as I moved in he wanted me to be his fucking maid. 'Don't you know how to cook?' he goes. Of course, does he know how to cook? No." Sandra sighed and shook her head. "Anyway, we would fight all the time and he would go out and not tell me where he was going and he'd constantly be on his phone and hide it from me if I came close. I figured he was seeing some other girl. So one day I followed him." Sandra was telling me this in a monotone, looking up at the ceiling. It was like she was seeing the events she was describing unfolding like a movie on my bedroom ceiling.

"He went down to Pape and Danforth and I see him go into this bar, so I stand across the street to see if he's meeting up with a girl. Well. No. He was not meeting a girl. Who's he meeting?" Sandra turned to look at me. The knowledge of what she was going to say next came to me a fraction of a second before she said it. I was about to form the name on my lips when she spoke.

"Brian." Sandra turned to look at the ceiling again. "I almost fell over when I saw him. All the time since Carly got shot I was trying to tell them it was Brian who shot her. That she was afraid of him and they pretended to think I was right and they were going to try to find him. Well, they found him sure enough and I could see him sitting at a table in a bar, talking together like old friends. They even did the bro hug thing. I couldn't believe it. I couldn't understand why Amir hadn't told me. I hated being left in the dark." Although she was saying that she was angry, Sandra's voice was getting quieter. She stopped talking for a minute, and I realized that she was falling asleep. I watched her eyes close and then her breathing became slow and regular. After a few minutes her legs twitched and she shifted positions, but she didn't wake up. While Sandra slept I went downstairs and cleaned up the dishes from the Thai food. The washing machine had finished so I put the clothes in the dryer.

Having Sandra show up when she did made me forget about the university letter for the moment. I figured I would deal with it once I had figured out what was going on with Sandra. It was early afternoon by then and Harold and Maggie weren't due home for hours. I didn't know how long Sandra would sleep for and I thought it was a bit creepy to sit and watch her sleep, so I stayed downstairs. Eventually I turned on the TV which was tuned, as usual, to the news channel since that is what Harold and Maggie would watch in the morning before going to work.

I sat numbly on the couch watching a piece on the Christmas Market and then the traffic report. There were lots of accidents even though it was only snowing lightly. Then the weather: snow would get heavier later and probably more accidents. I only half paid attention to what was being said so I didn't really hear what was being said before a familiar face appeared on the screen. It was Detective Aquino. She was being interviewed by a reporter standing in front of a small house with yellow police tape. I sat forward on the couch. "...investigation is at its early stages. We do have one deceased person, a female approximately fifty years of age. Anyone with information is asked to contact police." The reporter thanked Detective Aquino and then spoke to the news anchor.

The snow was causing the camera's lens to blur slightly and the reporter's nose was slightly red from the cold. "Neighbours tell us that a woman lived here alone, Mark. They say she was very friendly and would help out anyone in the neighbourhood. This is a tight-knit neighbourhood in Scarborough; one woman told us that everyone knew each other and that she knew the woman who lived here well. This woman did not want to be identified, Mark, but she told us that the woman who lived here, who we believe is the deceased, had recently taken in a nephew who had fallen on hard times." The reporter looked at her phone for her notes. "Police have not released the name of the deceased, they say they are in the process of notifying next of kin and trying to determine the circumstances that led to this person's death.

The shot returned to the anchor in the studio. "Thanks Tamia. We'll check in with you later." I turned off the TV. A deep feeling of dread emerged in the pit of my stomach. I knew somehow that the dead woman and Sandra's appearance on my doorstep were connected. I didn't know how, but I had a feeling when Sandra woke up, I would soon know.

The days were so short at that time of year that it was getting dark when Sandra woke up. I make her a cup of tea and she ate almost an entire package of cookies. We sat at the dining room table. The snow was starting to fall more heavily now and the temperature was dropping. "So turns out I was wrong about Brian." Sandra looked out the window into the backyard. She looked a little better after her nap, but she was nervous. Her hand shook as she held the mug of tea and she shifted uneasily in her chair.

"Did you get to talk to him?" I didn't want to pester her with questions. It was clear that she was there to talk. She would tell me everything.

"Yeah. I talked to him. He was nothing like I thought. I approached him that same day. The day I saw him with Amir. Amir left and Brian was still sitting in the bar just kind of looking out the window. I figured, what the hell? Obviously Amir wasn't telling me the truth so I may as well hear Brian's side of the story. You know, Frida, he was so straight with me. He told me everything that first day. After all Amir's lies and sneaking around it felt so good to just have someone tell me the truth, you know?" Sandra looked at me to make sure I understood how she felt. I nodded. I could see that talking to Brian had been a relief. What did he tell her?

"He told me all about Michal and Amir and the Albanians. They are crooks, Frida. They're into all kinds of bad stuff, but Brian knew mainly about how they would steal cars. It was this whole elaborate thing with tech devices to hack the alarm systems of specific cars that got taken for specific customers and then shipped to Italy and then like Dubai or something. Brian said that the whole thing started in Montreal and that Michal had double-crossed some guy he worked with there and had come to Toronto to start up his own ring.

"How did Brian know all this?"

"He was in jail with the Montreal guy's cousin."

"Why was he in jail?"

Sandra was talking quickly now and she got up and started pacing back and forth. "That's a whole other messed up story. His own mom got him arrested for assault. Which he didn't even do. She was just really horrible to him when they were kids. She always preferred Carly and would treat him like dirt."

I tried to picture Carly's mom from the funeral. I had a vague picture of a shaky, dark-haired woman in large sunglasses.

"Every little thing he would do wrong she would threaten to kick him out and she just made his whole life a misery. So he's in jail with this guy's cousin and he tells him the whole story and when he comes out he goes to live with his aunt 'cuz he can't take his mom any more."

"Did the aunt live in Toronto?"

"She had a little house in Scarborough. So anyway, he's trying to get his life together and he gets a gig picking up litter downtown. Kind of a community service type thing, but they paid him minimum wage. So, he's downtown picking up litter and he sees his buddy from jail. So after work they get together and his buddy tells him that his cousin in Montreal got a tip that Michal was seen hanging around in Yorkville and asked him to keep an eye out for him." Sandra was getting really agitated now and she leaned her hangs on the table and looked me right in the eyes. "So fucking Michal is running a car theft ring while eating pasta and drinking cappuccino on the patio at Bouillabaisse. Brian's buddy from jail shows Brian a picture of Michal and asks him to look out for him while he's doing his litter picking. Not only does Brian see Michal, he sees him with his sister, Carly!"

Sandra ran out of steam then. She sat down and rested her elbows on the table and held her head in her hands. "That's why Brian came looking for Carly. He came to warn her to stay away from Michal."

"Oh shit! But why was she so weird about seeing him?"

"Probably her mom filled her head with lies about Brian."

The pieces seemed to fit together, but it all came so fast I felt sure I wasn't getting the whole picture. "Where's Brian now?'

"That's the really messed up part, Frida. That's why I need your help." Sandra reached to grab my good hand. She held it tightly and I looked at her and saw my dearest friend. The one who had led me and been there for me. She needed me now.

"Whatever you need, Sandra, of course."

"I knew I could count on you." We clasped each other in a hug for a minute and then she continued her story. "After Carly got shot Brian didn't know what to think. He figured it had something to do with the Montreal guy, but he couldn't get in touch with his friend from jail and he didn't know how to figure out what had happened. He tries to ask around about Michal, but nobody knows anything. Then one guy tells him that he doesn't know Michal, but he does know another Albanian guy: Amir. So when I saw them together on the Danforth that day Brian had been trying to get close to Amir to see if he could find out anything more about the shooting."

"But did Amir know who did it?"

"Probably. But Brian never got close enough to find out anything and then that dude got arrested and Amir drops off the face of the earth."

"And were you living with Amir this whole time?"

"Yeah. Brian wanted to see if I could find anything out, but Amir got more and more cagey and then one day after the arrest, I get back from getting my nails done and he's packed up all his things and left. No explanation. Nothing. His number is out of service. No sign of Michal."

"So what did you do?"

"Well, I stayed in the apartment until I got evicted because I couldn't pay the rent. My mom can only send me money sometimes and its barely enough for food and phone bill."

"So where did you go?

"Brian said I could go stay with him at his aunt's place."

"I think I remember her. She was at the funeral."

Sandra stood up and turned her back to me. The snow had continued to fall and it was fully dark now. "Yeah. She was at the funeral. Brian said she was the only one in the family who ever gave him a chance." Sandra didn't say anything for a couple of minutes. "Can I borrow your phone charger?"

"Yeah sure." I had taken her phone out of her jeans pocket before putting them in the wash and I had noticed that it was completely dead. I grabbed it from the laundry room and my charger from my bedroom. "I'll plug it in here." I used the outlet near the kettle. Sandra nodded and come to stand by the counter to wait for the phone to come back to life. I could see that Sandra was not going to continue her story just then so I went to get my phone. There was a message from Costanza.

U good? I feel bad about what happened. Call me.

This felt like a message from another planet. I couldn't think about Costanza and Joey and Guelph. I didn't respond.

Sandra's phone had come back to life. She peered at the screen while biting her lower lip. "I gotta go." She stood up, but then hesitated. "Thanks for ..."

"Don't even mention it." I moved towards her and reached out my good hand to hold her wrist. "Where are you going?"

"I gotta go help Brian."

"Is he at his aunt's place still?" I tried to ask this question lightly since I felt like I knew the answer.

Sandra looked at me quickly. "No. We can't go back there." We've been staying down by the Gardiner. There's some shacks and tents there. But they are coming to clear it out, so we gotta move."

I was still holding Sandra's wrist. I squeezed it gently. "Why can't you go back to his aunt's place?"

Sandra pulled her arm away and covered her face with her hands. Her voice was shaky. "You don't understand. His mom turns everyone against him. Carly and then his aunt. He never would have hurt her on purpose. She was the only one who ever gave him a chance." Sandra's breathing was ragged and I could see the tears trickling through her fingers.

"What happened to Brian's aunt, Sandra?" I had a weird calmness like I was watching myself have this conversation.

Sandra went back to the window. It was dark and we had the lights on in the kitchen so she could see her own reflection more than anything outside. "She fell. I heard them arguing. Then I heard some kind of shuffling noises and then a thud." Sandra turned to look at me. "He never would have hurt her on purpose." I didn't know if she was trying to convince herself or me.

I gave Sandra what little cash I had. I gathered up some old blankets and sweaters that had belonged to Paul and put them in a bag. Sandra put her old clothes, clean now, back on and walked out the door. She hugged me before leaving. "Thank you so much. I'll text you later." I watched her walk down the street. The snow was tapering off now, but enough had fallen to turn the lawns and trees white. My phone pinged. Costanza again.

RU mad? Call me.

I thought of Costanza with her white board, her quick efficient movements and clear confident eyes. What the hell, I thought. I may as well call her.

"So you are alive." She picked up right away. I could hear dishes clattering and people talking in the background.

"Are you working?"

"When am I not working?"

"True." I stayed on the phone with Costanza for over an hour. Periodically she would yell something at someone else in the kitchen or tell me to hang on a minute while she drained some hot pasta or ran the blender. Mostly I just talked. I told her about failing most of my classes. I told her about drinking the vodka in the cloakroom with Joey.

"I knew you guys were up to something."

I told her about Luke. I told her about Arlene. "Holy shit, Frida. You've been carrying all that around? No wonder you're hitting the bottle."

The floodgates had opened and I wanted to tell her about Sandra, but I hesitated. The other stuff was in the past. This was now. Costanza had to go anyway. They were loading the van to go to the event. "Listen, Frida. You gotta go to student services in January. Ask for an appointment with a counsellor and tell them all this shit you just told me. They're going to give you a second chance. At least maybe they'll let you do some courses towards your degree."

"I don't know. Maybe university is not for me."

"Shut up. University is for you. You are smart. You just need to drink less and study more. Lots of people overdo it their first semester and they don't have the excuse you do, they're just idiots."

I had to laugh. I felt like Costanza had put me on her to-do list. "Fix Frida" We hung up the phone.

Harold and Maggie came home. I made sure there was no trace of Sandra having been there. "Did you eat all of that leftover Thai? Maggie stood looking into the fridge.

"Oh yeah, sorry. I was really hungry for some reason." Maggie looked at me and I left the kitchen before she saw right through me. I went up to my room. I looked up the news on my phone. Even though I was half expecting it, it was still a shock to see Brian's picture on the screen.

"Police have identified a person of interest in relation to the death of a woman in Scarborough ..." It was a mug shot. Seeing Brian's face on the screen made me feel cold all over. What had Sandra gotten herself into? I didn't go downstairs for dinner. Maggie said that she wasn't surprised given that I had eaten all that Thai food. Of course I hadn't eaten any of it and I was actually quite hungry, but I didn't think I could fake being okay for an entire family dinner. I didn't hear the doorbell ring because I had put music on to distract me while I waited for Sandra's text. Maggie came to my room. Her face was tense. "Frida. That police detective is here, Detective Aquino. She wants to talk to you." My heart was in my throat. I tried to appear calm.

"Okay. Tell her I'll be right down." I didn't know what I would say. I just went downstairs and saw Detective Aquino standing in the front hall. She had a dark grey coat on and her hair was tied back. Just like when I had met her before, she wore no makeup and small gold earrings. She looked relaxed which made me relax too.

"Hi Frida, how have you been?"

"Yeah, great. What's going on?"

"Can we talk? I'm hoping you can help with something."

Harold and Maggie said that they would go upstairs so that we could talk privately. Maggie asked Detective Aquino if she wanted anything to drink. Detective Aquino refused politely and waited in silence while they went upstairs. We sat at the dining room table. Exactly where Sandra had been earlier that evening. "I'm not sure if you saw the news?" Detective Aquino took out her notebook and a pen. Her voice was casual, like she was asking whether I had seen the hockey game. I nodded. My throat felt swollen and I didn't trust myself to talk.

"We think Sandra and Brian may be together. I was wondering whether Sandra might have reached out to you?" In the interminable three seconds that elapsed between Detective Aquino asking me that question and me answering a million things went through my mind. Sandra telling Steve to leave me alone. Alex telling me off for not speaking up for Lionel. Carly lying on the floor of the restaurant with blood spreading over her chest. Luke breaking a flowerpot over Nick's head while Arlene watched with baby me in a stroller. Then Sandra again, as she had been tonight with tears coming through her fingers. I didn't have time to organize those images and thoughts into anything that made sense. I didn't make a decision to lie and cover for Brian and Sandra. The next thing I said came out automatically.

"I haven't been in touch with Sandra since Carly's funeral. I don't think she would be with Brian. She always hated him."

Detective Aquino nodded. She seemed to believe me. "I hope you are right. Brian is a very troubled individual." She wrote something in her notebook.

"What do you mean, troubled?"

Detective Aquino looked at me. Her face was calm, but there was a tightness around her mouth that made me think she was holding something back. "Frida, I'm only telling you this because if your friend is involved with Brian and if she does reach out to you, you should tell her to get away from him and turn herself in to police right away." She put her notebook away and took out her phone. She started scrolling through her phone as she talked. "Brian has been involved with police since he was eleven years old. He was kicked out of multiple schools.

He had numerous charges for various offences. His mom tried everything to help him. He would promise to do better and go to some programs and counselling, but a couple of months later he would be back at it. Finally when he was seventeen she had enough. She was afraid for herself and for Carly. She told him he had to move out." Detective Aquino had been scrolling her phone the whole time she had been telling me this. She stopped now and turned the phone towards me. It was a picture of a woman with dark hair. I didn't recognize who it was, but that was not surprising since her face was so badly bruised and cut up it could have been Maggie and I wouldn't have recognized her. "This is Brian's and Carly's mom. This is what he did to her when she told him he had to move out."

I looked at the woman's face. I supposed that this could have been the woman I saw at the funeral. "Did Brian hurt Carly too?"

"We don't think so. There was never any report of that."

"And you still think he had nothing to do with her shooting?"

Detective Aquino sighed. "That situation was extremely complex. We are confident that we got the shooter thanks to your testimony, but we know there is a larger story there and we believe Brian may have been involved in some way."

I didn't know what to say or think. Was Sandra right to trust Brian? Maybe she was in over her head and I needed to help her out. Was Detective Aquino just making up that stuff about Brian because they wanted someone to blame for his aunt's death. I could see that Detective Aquino had her mind made up about Brian. Even if his aunt's death had been an accident they would never believe him.

Detective Aquino took out a card and gave it to me. "It's a lot to take in, I know. If Sandra does get in touch, call me. I want to help her, but if she is helping Brian evade police she is committing a crime."

I knew that Detective Aquino was trying to tell me that if I helped Sandra help Brian evade police, I was also committing a crime. I took the card without saying anything. Detective Aquino stood up and went towards the door. She called up to Harold and Maggie, "we're done here. Thanks so much and sorry for the intrusion." I let her out and closed the door behind her. My heart was racing and my mouth felt dry. I heard my phone ping. It was Sandra. I didn't have a chance to read the message because Harold and Maggie were coming downstairs with concerned faces. I felt a rush of tenderness for them as they came down the stairs. They seemed to move a little tentatively, and for the first time I thought about them as old. This was all the more reason to protect them from everything that was going on. I didn't want them to worry. Lying to Detective Aquino had come automatically, but I made a conscious effort to act happy and carefree for Harold and Maggie.

"Don't look so worried. I'm not getting arrested tonight!" I put on a smile and went to the kitchen. I knew Maggie would relax if she saw me eating so I went into the fridge and took out a yogurt.

"What did the detective want?"

"Just some questions about other people from Bouillabaisse. I didn't know anything so I couldn't really help."

"We had no idea that restaurant job was going to involve you in so much danger, Frida. We never would have let you go work there if we had known." Maggie cut a banana in half and placed it beside me on the table, wordlessly continuing her quest to get me to eat all the fruit and vegetables she believed I had not eaten in Guelph.

"It's a weird thing. I didn't know any of that stuff was going on when I was working there. I feel kind of dumb, actually, that I didn't know."

Harold sat across from me at the table. He looked tired. "I'm not surprised you didn't know, Frida. You're a good person.

When you look around you, you see good. Unfortunately, when you have a little more experience, you'll see that there's quite a bit of bad too. The trick is knowing how to tell the good from the bad. It's not always easy." Harold stood up and went to the corner cupboard. I watched him reach in behind Maggie's china and retrieve the hidden whiskey bottle. Maggie raised her eyebrows at him. "Really, Harold? Is it as bad as all that?" She spoke teasingly.

Harold got three glasses and poured a small serving of whiskey for each of us. We raised our glasses. "To you, Frida. I hope you always see the good and learn how to avoid the bad in life." I wished that this had been my first time drinking whiskey. I wished I didn't have to pretend to find the taste harsh. I wished that Harold's evaluation of me was correct. That I was a good person. He was definitely correct about one thing. It wasn't easy to tell the good from the bad.

I finally looked at the text from Sandra.

Tent city getting cleared tomorrow. B says we can stay with a friend in Brampton. Can U drive us?

Harold and Maggie had said that I could use the Honda if I wanted, but how could I drive with a broken wrist? I hadn't driven since the summer and I had never driven to Brampton.

"Can't drive all the way to Brampton with broken wrist."

"Shit. I forgot about your wrist." No reply for a few minutes. "B says he can drive to Brampton if you can get the car down here."

How was I going to explain this to Harold and Maggie? I hadn't left the house since returning from Guelph and now on a random snowy Tuesday night I was going to take the car and be gone for hours?

"I'll come after Harold and Maggie are asleep."

"Okay. Thanks. You are a life saver."

This gave me a couple of hours to think.

UNDER THE GARDINER

The noise of the Gardiner was constant. The snow had no chance to stick to surfaces down here, the heat and friction of vehicles maintained the grey black roads. Sandra had described the location of the tent city and I caught a glimpse of a bright blue tarp that formed part of one of the shelters. At first it looked abandoned. You might think it was a pile of debris from a construction site. I stood on the other side of Lakeshore Boulevard for a minute just looking at it and getting up my nerve. I didn't hear footsteps approaching so I jumped a little when a voice came from behind me.

"Not such a great place to live, eh?"

I put my hand to my heart. "You scared me!"

"Sorry. Didn't mean to sneak up on you like that." It was a young girl. She couldn't have been more than fourteen years old. Her dark, straight hair was cut in a non-style that made me think she had done it herself, or maybe her mom. She was wearing a hoodie and jean jacket, jeans and black running shoes.

"Do you live there?" She was standing close enough to me that I would have been able to smell that sour, unwashed smell that Sandra had brought with her. This girl didn't have that, and she didn't have a hungry look either. Her cheeks were full and her eyes were clear. She stood still without the shakes and jitters I had seen with Sandra.

"No. I don't live there. I just come down to talk to some of the old folks here sometimes."

"By yourself?" In spite of her confidence she was just a child.

"Yeah."

"What about your parents?"

She turned her head to look down the street. She was preparing to cross. Not to run away from me and my question, I felt. Just because it was time. "My parents?" She looked back at me. "Oh. They have problems of their own." She said this like she felt sorry for them, but that the problems of her parents were not her concern, just as the fact that she was going to visit some old people at a tent city under the Gardiner was no concern of her parents'.

I watched her cross the street and duck into the tent city. I tried to take in some of her calmness and composure. A child with a clear-eyed understanding of what to do, of how to be in the world. I took out my phone.

I'm here. On Lakeshore. Come out.
Are you in the car?
No. On foot. Come by yourself.

After a couple of minutes Sandra came out. She looked around nervously until she spotted me. She came across to where I was standing. "What are you doing? Where is the car?"

"Sandra. We need to talk for a minute."

"Why? Don't tell me you're backing out. I got nowhere else to turn, Frida." Sandra's voice was shaky and her eyes were full of fear.

"Are you sure about Brian, Sandra? I mean, how well do you really know him? You're taking a huge risk."

"Don't you think I know I'm taking a risk? I don't care. What have I got to lose? Brian took a risk with me. I can't leave him high and dry now."

"Listen, Sandra. I've got $200 cash. Why don't you just give him the money and then come home with me. He'll figure shit out and you can stay with me until your mom gets back or whatever."

"And what are you gonna do? Quit university to look after me until I get my shit together? No Frida. That's no good. Why don't you believe me? Brian is a good guy. He just needs someone to give him a chance."

"I thought his aunt gave him a chance. Look what happened to her."

Sandra was stung. "I feel terrible about his aunt, okay? But there's nothing I can do about that now. Why don't you at least come and talk to Brian? See for yourself. If you don't like him, you can go your own way and just forget this whole thing. Please Frida. You owe me that at least."

Brian and Sandra had been sleeping in a shack made of plywood, metal sheeting and tarps. It was only moderately warmer inside than outside and the smell made my eyes sting. Brian was sitting with his legs stretched out in front of him. He filled most of the space with his body and energy. When Sandra and I came in we both squeezed into a corner and sat cross-legged.

Brian studied me without emotion. I remembered his face from the mug shot on the news and the funeral. I tried not to show how nervous I was. "So you're Frida."

Sandra tried to warm things up. "I told Brian all about us. How we grew up together and everything."

"That's nice that you guys are still friends." Brian's face when he said this changed just slightly from the emotionless mask. He softened just around his eyes and he looked at Sandra in a way that I could see he really cared for her. "So I guess you knew Carly too?"

"Yeah. We worked together. The three of us."

"And you were there the night of the shooting?"

"Yeah, I was there."

"That was some messed up shit." Brian bent his knees and sat up slightly. He wrapped his arms around his knees and intertwined the fingers of his hands, turning them away from himself so that his knuckles cracked loudly. "So. Where'd you park the car?"

Harold was sitting in the Honda parked about five minutes walk away. I had told him some of the truth, leaving out the part about Brian. He was expecting me to come back with Sandra who I had told him needed a place to stay.

I looked at Brian. When he had bent his knees, his pants rode up on his leg slightly and I could see the handle of a knife sticking out from the top of his right boot. I took a deep breath. "It's not far. Five minutes away."

"Alright. Let's go."

Sandra and I unfolded ourselves and left the shack. Brian was rummaging around, gathering up his few belongings. "Sandra, I really need to pee. I guess there's no bathroom here?"

"No, Frida. You can go behind the blue tarp. It's really gross, but just hold your breath."

I walked towards the blue tarp that Sandra had indicated. As I passed other makeshift shelters and tents I could hear movements and groans from within. A low laugh from one. Snoring from another. I made the call as quickly as I could and went back towards Sandra. I really did need to pee, but there was no time for that now.

Brian was almost a foot taller than Sandra and when he put his arm around her shoulder she seemed so small. I walked besides them, trying to go as slowly as I could.

"I guess you heard they arrested someone for Carly's shooting?" Brian looked over Sandra's head at me. We had left the tent city now and were crossing north away from the Gardiner. The streetlights made it light enough to see clearly where we were going but not light enough to read the expression on Brian's face. His tone was neutral. Was he testing me?

"Yeah. I heard that."

"Cops always have to arrest someone to make it look like they are keeping things under control." Brian scoffed. "They don't know shit. They have no fucking idea what is really going on.'

"Really? I thought the guy pleaded guilty."

"They trick you into pleading guilty. It's such a crock of shit. Believe me."

"But I heard that there were witnesses and stuff." What made me challenge Brian on this, I don't know. We had crossed Lakeshore and were heading towards where Harold was sitting in the Honda. We probably had two minutes. I hoped it would be enough.

"What do you know about it?" Brian had stopped walking. Maybe I could keep us here for a little longer.

"Well. I just heard that there were witnesses that night who ID'ed the shooter. That's all."

"And who did you hear this from?" Brian stood looking at me.

"Why the hell are we talking about this now?" Sandra put her hand on Brian's arm. "We gotta get moving."

Brian shook her off. "I just wanna hear what Frida knows about my sister getting shot. Seems like she knows more than what she's saying."

"You don't know anything, do you Frida?" Sandra looked at me pleadingly.

"All I'm saying is that the cops said they had a witness, that's all."

"The cops said?" Brian took a step towards me. "The cops said this to who? To you?"

In spite of the cold I could feel sweat gathering under my arms. I had to hold my jaw to keep my teeth from chattering with fear. "No. Not to me specifically. I just heard that they did."

"You know what I think, Sandra?" Brian put his arm back around Sandra's shoulder. "I think your friend here likes the smell of bacon. She's a fucking cop lover. Aren't you Frida?" He said this half jokingly, but I knew it was no joke.

"I don't love cops. I'm just saying it seems like they got the right guy for Carly's shooting."

Brian moved quickly. He reached into his boot, grabbed my arms from behind and held the knife to my throat. Sandra screamed. "What the hell, Brian!"

Brian whispered into my ear, "You don't know shit about Carly's shooting and you don't know shit about me. You called the cops on us, didn't you? You cop-loving piece of shit."

I looked down the street. I could see Harold walking towards us. He must have heard Sandra's scream. He had his phone to his ear.

"I don't know what you're talking about. I didn't call the cops. I'm just here to help Sandra." My arms were pinned behind me and the flat of the knife blade was pressing into my windpipe so that I was having trouble breathing.

"Shut up!" He yanked my arms and pain shot through my already broken wrist. I felt like passing out.

Sandra was crying. "Brian, what are you doing? She hasn't done anything. She just trying to help us, baby."

"No Sandra. Your little friend here is a traitor. She's working with the cops. I could smell pig as soon as I saw her."

The siren sound and the lights and the cops yelling "Drop your weapon!" all came then. I could see Sandra standing still as a statue in the coloured lights of the police car. She looked at me with disbelief as she and Brian were handcuffed. I was taken to an ambulance where a paramedic checked me out. He was a gentle guy with dark skin and an accent. He calmly took my pulse, wrapped me in a blanket and said that my wrist would probably need to be reset.

Detective Aquino came over. "Frida. You okay?"

I couldn't speak. I just shook my head.

"Can I bring your Dad over?" I could see Harold standing in the background, but when she said Dad strangely Luke came to mind. I could see him in his brown DFC hat and sunburned arms. Detective Aquino brought Harold over. He hugged me gently, trying not to hurt my arm. I just cried and told Harold "I'm so sorry" over and over again.

"It's going to be okay, Frida. You're safe now."

*   *   *

When the world closed down for Coronavirus it was a relief. I had returned to Guelph. Costanza had taken me for my counselling appointment and they didn't need to hear even half my story before they granted me special consideration and let me register as a part time student and offered me regular counselling support. Harold and Maggie tried to not be too overprotective, but they couldn't help but look anxious. They even talked about moving to Guelph. I told them that was not necessary. I told them about Luke and tried to make him sound more like a responsible adult and less like ... Luke.

It was a struggle. I had decided to quit drinking. Classes were hard. Costanza was so bossy. Every tall blonde guy was Brian and I would break into a sweat if one came near me.

Being back in North York under lockdown was peaceful. I did my school work in my old room with my picture of Lionel and Teresa and the allotment garden gang. By April some days were warm. I would go for walks in the ravine. It was magical to leave the car-lined streets and descend into the green coolness. The smells in the ravine were delicious. The creek, the earth, the fresh grasses and emerging leaves.

Some days I would look ahead of me into a curve in the path and imagine that Sandra was there just beyond the curve. I imagined her turning to greet me and I imagined that we would walk and talk together and straighten everything out. This idea made me smile.

Manufactured by Amazon.ca
Bolton, ON

33565396R00139